Fish Fry

Jill Watson Glassco

Deep Sea Publishing, LLC

Copyright Page

Printed in the USA

ISBN-13: 978-1-939535-49-8
ISBN: 1-939535-49-2

Table of Contents

For:

Fisher

"Ask and you shall receive." (Matthew 7:7)

Chapter 1:

Missing

Professor Sparrow vanishing into thin air raised more fuss and feathers than the time Mrs. Alice Holtshausen plowed down the cemetery gates in old Gertie — her 1987 Lincoln Town Car.

"I thought surely to goodness Gertie could squeeze right through there," she told the Monroe County deputy.

Mrs. Alice and Professor Sparrow were both old as dirt, maybe older. Her ancestors were among the founding fathers of Clear Creek, a small community in southern Indiana. Sparrow had moved there in 1978 as the new history professor at Indiana University over in Bloomington. Mrs. Alice's great-great-grandfather's mansion happened to be on the market at the time. The professor snatched it up sight unseen.

The sheriff was still scratching his head trying to figure whether the missing professor was truly in peril or just pulling a prank — like the history riddle he used to give his students every semester, promising an "A" to whomever solved the puzzle. After a kid named Jacob Fickle helped an IU freshman unravel the old man's secret kept under hat for forty years, it ended the game but launched a friendship between the professor and the boys. Peril or prank, Professor Sparrow's whereabouts had Clear Creek buzzing like a hornets' nest . . .

Friday 3:27 P.M.

"Fifty-one, fifty-two, fifty-three." Isaac Fickle juggled the soccer ball from knee to foot to head.

Friday afternoons, like country fried chicken and peaches, made the boy's list of "Things That Make Me Happy."

7

"Fifty-four, fifty-five, fifty . . . "

Out of the blue, a big hand snatched the ball from midair and hurled it toward the trampoline.

"Hey," Isaac yelled. "Whatya do that for, Jacob?"

Isaac watched his sixteen-year-old brother run in the shed and ride out on a bicycle. Jacob topped his "People Who Pick on Me" list.

"Where you going?" Isaac asked.

"Professor Sparrow's."

"Can I go?"

"I'm in a hurry."

"I'll keep up. Just let me grab my bike."

"Suit yourself, Fish Fry." Jacob took off without him and sped down Mulberry Street.

Isaac hollered, "Isaac! My name's Isaac!"

At twelve, Isaac had decided to drop the embarrassing "Fish Fry" nickname. His mom loved telling his friends the story — Jacob had taken one look at the red-faced, newly born brother and said he looked like a fish fry. He meant french fry, but the label stuck like a worm on a hook. Kids at school called him names like Fish Stick or Fishy Man. Isaac didn't like being teased.

Two Monroe County Sheriff cars blocked Professor Sparrow's tall gates. Jacob and his friends clustered behind blue, flashing lights.

Isaac dropped his bike and checked his watch. *Nine minutes and thirty-nine seconds*, he thought. *Fourteen seconds faster than last time.*

"What's up?" he called.

Caleb, Jacob's best friend since the fifth grade, nodded toward the timeworn mansion shrouded by oak trees. "Sparrow's missing."

Isaac frowned. "Missing? Whatcha mean missing?"

Dustin, the "new guy" even though he had moved to town three years ago, smirked. "What part of *missing* do you not understand, kid?"

The boys laughed. Isaac's face burned beet red.

"Professor Sparrow hasn't been to class all week and look." Caleb pointed to the overflowing mailbox. "The mailman called the cops."

Jacob stared at the house. "This is awful. I gotta do something."

"Whatcha gonna do?" Isaac asked.

"You guys wait here. I'll be back in a minute."

Caleb and Dustin shot a thumbs up as Jacob stole through the gates and slipped up a path between the iron fence and shaggy bushes.

Isaac followed. "Are you crazy?"

"Shhh. I'm just gonna check the tunnel," Jacob whispered. "Professor Sparrow might be down there hurt or something."

"Tell the police," Isaac said in a low voice, but Jacob kept moving. *Here we go*, he thought. Visions of trouble danced in his head.

The brothers sneaked up the hill. Jacob peered through bushes then jerked back like a turtle in a shell. He made a gun with his thumb and finger and pointed toward the house.

Isaac mouthed, "What?"

Jacob rolled his eyes and, with a stick, scratched "cops" in the dirt.

This is a bad idea, Isaac thought, *a really, really bad idea.*

When the coast cleared, the boys crept across the lawn to the back porch. Isaac glanced over both shoulders. "How we gonna get in?"

"You'll see." Jacob tilted a flowerpot and grabbed the key underneath.

"No, Jacob! That's breaking and entering."

"No, it's not. Professor Sparrow showed me this key and told me to use it anytime."

Jacob unlocked the backdoor. They tiptoed into the shadowy kitchen. A crumpled newspaper and half-filled coffee cup sat on the table. Dirty dishes piled the white porcelain sink. Without warning, voices rumbled from the living room.

Isaac's eyes grew to saucers. His heart pounded with the tick-tock, tick-tock of the gingerbread clock on the faded floral wallpaper. In his mind, SWAT stormed the kitchen with bazookas the size of canons. He shuddered. *We're toast.*

Jacob grabbed a flashlight from the top of the old Frigidaire and motioned for Isaac to follow. They inched over the black and white checkerboard tiles to the cellar door and pulled.

C-R-E-A-K!

The brothers froze like deer in headlights.

Tick-tock.

13

Tick-tock.

Tick-tock.

No SWAT swarmed. So, the boys skulked down the stairs.

"Over here," Jacob whispered. He lifted a dusty, cotton rag rug. "Trapdoor to the tunnel."

Isaac fanned the dust. "We're (cough) not supposed to go down there without an adult."

"It's okay. I'll just be a minute. Wait here."

Isaac shook his head hard. "No way! You're not leaving me here all by myself. I'm going, too."

A rope ladder dangled from the opening. It swayed like the kitchen clock pendulum as Jacob disappeared into the darkness.

"Okay, come on down."

Isaac's legs felt like silly string.

"Hurry up, Fish Fry."

"But . . . the ladder . . . "

Jacob pulled it taut. "Don't worry. I got it."

Isaac felt for the first rung. The ladder swung.
"Hold it still, Jacob!"

"I'm trying!"

One . . .

Two . . .

Three . . .

It fell like climbing down a metronome.

Keep moving, Isaac told himself.

Four . . .

Five . . .

The descent seemed a mile long.

Six . . .

Next step his foot hit hard-packed clay. The cool
air smelled like dirt.

Jacob threw light down the timber-framed shaft.

"Professor Sparrow, you down here?"

A blinding light suddenly filled the tunnel.

"Freeze!!!"

Jacob's flashlight hit the floor. Isaac's knees buckled.

"Put your hands over your heads!"

REFLECTIONS

POINT TO PONDER

When the boys learned that Professor Sparrow was

_____, they searched for him. Have you

ever lost something or someone important to you? What

did you lose?

PEARL FROM GOD

Jesus told this story, "If a man has a hundred sheep and one

of them gets lost, what will he do? Won't he leave the ninety-

nine others in the wilderness and go search for the one that is

lost until he finds it?" (Luke 15:3-4 NLT)

PRINCIPLE TO LIVE BY

Jesus is our Great Shepherd. In His goodness and steadfast

love, He chases after lost people (those far from God) all the

days of their lives, inviting them to trust Him and dwell in

His kingdom forever. Trust Jesus, beloved, your great and

faithful Shepherd.

Chapter 2:

Wiser Than a Sixth Grader

5:17 P.M.

Elizabeth was sketching Eva Mozes Kor, a lady she once met at the CANDLES Holocaust Museum who had survived Auschwitz, when a car pulled into the driveway.

"Hey, Mom, a sheriff's car's here," she yelled.

From the kitchen, Mrs. Fickle heard her fourteen-year-old daughter giggle. "Jacob and Isaac are climbing out of the backseat!"

"What???" Mrs. Fickle was running now. She flew down the stairs and jerked open the front door into the face of Deputy Lou Carson.

He grinned. "Hey, Rebekah. Found a couple of strays over at Sparrow's place. Thought you might wanna take 'em in."

She peered over the deputy's shoulder. I-can't-believe-we-got-caught painted Jacob's face. I-told-you-not-to-do-it darkened Isaac's.

Mrs. Fickle shook her head. "Thanks, Lou. Where were they *exactly*?"

"In the tunnel."

Her jaw dropped. "What???"

Deputy Carson laughed and slapped Jacob on the back. "Better pray for mercy, son. See you guys at church on Sunday."

On Sunday, October sunlight blazed the stained-glass windows at Hebron Community Church. Isaac held one side of a hymnal. A crinkled hand gripped the other side. The boy and Mrs. Alice had shared a pew and hymnal ever since he found her sitting alone a few years back. The congregation warbled:

"God of mercy, God of grace,

Show the brightness of Thy face.

Shine upon us, Savior, shine,

Fill Thy church with light divine,

And Thy saving health extend

Unto earth's remotest end."[1]

Mrs. Alice sang every word of all three stanzas, never glancing once at hymn #297. Isaac was amazed. He loved music. Kids at school sometimes called him "hummingboy" because he sang all the time. An old family video showed toddler Isaac singing to Jesus, hands raised toward heaven.

Across the aisle, Jacob sandwiched between their mom and dad instead of friends — a light consequence for

---

[1] GOD OF MERCY, GOD OF GRACE. Henry Francis Lyte, 1834.

going in the tunnel without permission or a parent, and God's answer to prayers for mercy.

Come Monday, "IU Professor Missing" headlined every Indiana television, social media, and radio newscast as well as newspapers. The search had outgrown the Monroe County Sheriff's department. State troopers and FBI agents were now on hunt like hounds on a fox.

Before school that morning, Jacob and Mark Williams had their heads together, concocting their own search and rescue plan: deploying teammates from IU's track team and Clear Creek High School's soccer team. After school, an army of boys combed every crack and crevice of the town, woods, and neighboring farms.

Isaac considered tagging along, but fresh memories of the backseat of a patrol car nipped that notion in the bud.

His brother seemed to thrive on trouble; he avoided it like the plague.

Isaac checked the time: 3:41 P.M.

"Hey, Mom, can I go see Mrs. Alice?" he asked.

"Well, of course, but why, Fish Fry?"

The boy groaned. "Mom! I've told you a hundred times. *Isaac.* Call me Isaac."

"I'm sorry. I keep forgetting. So, why do you want to visit Mrs. Alice, Fi . . . uh, Isaac?"

"Well . . . I noticed there's a bunch of leaves in her yard, and I thought I'd go rake 'em for her."

"Such a good heart," Mrs. Fickle said and hugged him tight.

Guilt squeezed tighter. *I'll rake after I ask her,* he promised himself.

4:13 P.M.

Isaac unlatched the gate. White paint peeled from the picket fence like skin from a snake's back. Last summer's flowers withered under falling leaves. *Man, summertime passed by so fast it felt like we ran over the speed limit,* he thought.

A double-backed swing hung at one corner of the wrap-around porch. Mrs. Alice's late husband, James Whitcomb Holtzhausen (named for the Hoosier poet James Whitcomb Riley) designed the second back of the swing to roll forward, making a cradle for four babies and a passel of grandkids.

Mr. J. W., as everyone called him, had built the cozy cottage in 1957 as a wedding gift for his pretty, young bride, Miss Alice McCarthy, the town's librarian. He served as Clear Creek's postmaster for fifty-three years till God, the

Master of masters, called "Return to Sender." Townsfolk

filed through the cemetery for weeks to read his epitaph:

James Whitcomb Holtzhausen

Dedicated husband, father, and postmaster

April 4, 1926 — September 10, 2008

"Neither snow nor rain nor heat of day

Nor gloom of night could keep away

This mailman from appointed round.

A finer man could not be found.

An empty parcel lies below.

For straight to heaven, he did go."

May the Lord watch between us, dear, until we meet again.

Isaac knocked. A second knock brought footsteps.

Mrs. Alice's face lit up like a Christmas tree. "Isaac!

What a delightful surprise. Come on in, child. Your timing is impeccable. I just took a buttermilk pound cake out of the oven and was wishing for company."

Isaac followed her and a heavenly aroma to the kitchen.

"Have a seat. I'll cut us both a slice. Butter?"

"Yes, please."

"What nice manners." She pulled a silver butterknife from a drawer. "Nothing better than hot cake with melted butter. Would you like a glass of cold milk to wash it down?"

"Yes, thank you."

Mrs. Alice handed him a double-wide wedge on a pink rose china plate. "So, what brings you here today?"

"Well, I noticed there's lots of leaves in your yard and uh . . . I uh . . . I came to rake 'em for you." Her twinkling, green eyes met his blue ones. Isaac looked down. "And truth is . . . I wanted to ask you something."

She eased into the chair beside him. "Ask away,

child."

"You know Professor Sparrow's missing?"

"Yes, I know."

"Well, I wondered if . . . if you would help me find

him?"

"*Me* help *you* find Ben Sparrow?"

"Yes, ma'am."

"For goodness' sake, Isaac, why me? Why not Jacob or your friends?"

"Well, Jacob thinks I'm still a little kid, and . . . and sometimes he does stuff without thinking."

She chuckled. "You mean he leaps before he looks?"

"Exactly!" Next thing Isaac knew, he was spilling out the whole tunnel fiasco. Mrs. Alice leaned forward, listening attentively.

"You helped Jacob and Mark find the tunnels. So, I hoped maybe you'd help me find Professor Sparrow. And besides, you're a *lot* older and wiser . . . I mean . . . "

She laughed. "No cause to back out of that ditch, child. It's true. I'm old as the hills and wiser than most sixth graders — present company excluded, of course."

He gave a half grin. "And if I . . . if *we* find the professor, it'd show Jacob . . ." Isaac pulled at a loose thread on his jeans. "It's kinda hard being the baby of the family. Everybody's always . . . always . . . "

"Taller and stronger?"

"Yes, ma'am. And braver."

Mrs. Alice patted his freckled cheek. "Your day's coming, child. Your day's coming." She laughed. "When my boys were kids, the oldest was always picking on the little one. I'd say, 'You better be nice. He'll grow.' Well, one day, when they were teenagers, I heard Sam holler, 'Mama, make him stop!' When I came around the corner, Joe had his big brother pinned to the carpet. I said, 'I told you this day would come.'"

Isaac imagined pinning Jacob to the ground.

Mrs. Alice studied his face. "You know what?"

"What?"

"Maybe we can find Ben Sparrow. Partners?"

The boy smiled. "Partners!" he said and shook the blue-veined hand.

Mrs. Alice rose to her feet. "Enjoy your cake. I'll be right back."

REFLECTIONS

POINT TO PONDER

Isaac said Mrs. Alice was older and _____ than his friends. Who is the wisest person you know? Do you ever ask them for help or advice?

PEARL FROM GOD

"Oh, the depth of the riches of the wisdom and knowledge of God! How unsearchable His judgments, and His paths beyond tracing out!" (Romans 11:33)

PRINCIPLE TO LIVE BY

James 1:5 says: *"If you lack wisdom, you should ask God, who gives generously to all without finding fault, and it will be given to you."* Beloved, you need God's wisdom. I need God's wisdom. Every living soul needs God's wisdom. Why not ask God for His wisdom today?

Chapter 3:
Real Trouble

Isaac looked around the kitchen. *It's like Professor Sparrow's house,* he thought, *only happier.* Sunbeams through a window framed in yellow curtains painted bright puddles on the tiled floor. A German Black Forest cuckoo clock that Mr. J. W. had brought home from World War II hung near the window. Isaac checked its time, then glanced at his watch. *Two minutes slow,* he noted.

Outside, a cherry-red cardinal sat on a wooden feeder cracking sunflower seeds. A brown bird with red-tinged wings, tail, and crest perched beside him.

"The red one's Peppermint."

Isaac jumped. "You startled me. I didn't hear you come back."

"And the brown one's Butterscotch. They're mates."

"Do you name all the birds?" Isaac asked.

"Just my regular visitors."

Peppermint passed a seed from his beak to Butterscotch. "Did you see that?" Isaac cried. "He's feeding her!"

"It's called courtship feeding."

"If I were a bird," Isaac said, "I'd love to live by Wendy's and eat all the french fries people dropped."

Mrs. Alice laughed.

Isaac watched Peppermint fly away. "And if I were a bird and I had a brain, I'd do all kinds of things."

"What would you do?" she asked.

"I'd visit New Zealand."

"And if I were a bird, I'd go with you!" Mrs. Alice said.

A small yellow bird with black wings lit on the windowsill. "Who's that?" Isaac asked.

"That little goldfinch is Lemon Drop — named after my grandmother's favorite candy."

"It looks like a canary," Isaac said and wondered if he would name birds when he got old, and would getting old be sad, and did Mrs. Alice feel sad and lonely sometimes.

She seemed to read his mind. "The days can get awfully long and lonesome between visits from my family, but my feathered friends and Jesse James are good company. They keep me busy."

"Who's Jesse James?"

She pointed to a wad of leaves at the top of the oak holding the feeder. "That thieving squirrel that lives right up there. I have to fill the feeder two and three times a day because of his voracious appetite. Here." She dropped an envelope by Isaac's empty plate.

"What's this?"

"Ben Sparrow left it a couple of weeks ago. He asked me to give it to one of you boys if there was trouble."

Isaac's face fell. "He probably meant Jacob or Mark."

"No, actually, he said to give it to the one who asked for help. You asked, so there you go, honey."

"Can I open it?"

"By all means. Please do! I'm as curious as a cat to know what's in there."

On cue, a black and gray tabby sauntered into the kitchen and rubbed a fluffy back against Isaac's jeans.

"Morton!" Isaac cried. "I forgot all about you. Mrs. Alice, how did Professor Sparrow's cat get over here?"

"As soon as I learned Ben was missing, Gertie and I scooted over to the old mansion and brought Morton home with us."

"How'd you get in?"

She winked. "Jacob's not the only one who knows about that key under the flowerpot."

Isaac scratched Morton's head. The cat purred like a new Rolls-Royce.

Mrs. Alice nodded toward the envelope. "Aren't you going to open it?"

"Yes, ma'am!" He broke the seal and pulled out a folded paper.

"For heaven's sake, child, what does it say?"

He read aloud:

> "Joyful are those who listen to me,
>
> Watching for me daily at my gates,
>
> Waiting for me outside my home.
>
> For whoever finds me finds life."

The boy's brow crinkled. "What does that mean?"

Mrs. Alice shook her head.

"You think it's a clue to help us find him?" Isaac asked.

"Could be."

"What did he mean by *if* there's trouble?"

"You know Ben. Always mysterious."

"So, this isn't a joke. Professor Sparrow really is in trouble, and he knew something bad was about to happen."

Mrs. Alice sang, "Troublesome times are here, filling men's hearts with fear. Freedom we all hold dear now is at stake."

"Mrs. Alice, do you know *all* the words to *every* hymn?"

She threw her head back and cackled. "Not all, child, not all, but quite a few. I've had a long time to practice."

Isaac frowned. "I hope Professor Sparrow's okay."

Mrs. Alice patted his hand. "He's okay."

"How can you be so sure?"

She put a hand over her heart. "Because I feel it in here, and I know that Jesus is with him. Never fear trouble, child. It's the soil from which God grows courageous warriors."

"What do you mean?"

"I mean no pain no gain. Have you ever heard of the Apostle Paul?"

Isaac nodded.

"In his letter to the Corinthians, Paul described terrible troubles. He'd been shipwrecked, beaten, robbed, freezing cold, starved half to death, and overwhelmed beyond his ability to endure. He said he expected to die but ended up learning a valuable lesson. You know what he learned?"

Isaac shook his head.

"Paul learned to stop relying on himself and to depend completely on God. He put full confidence in the Lord, which gave him the strength and courage to finish God's work even in the face of persecution and imprisonment."

Isaac sat quietly. Mrs. Alice carried their dirty dishes to the sink. The clock door opened. A tiny, blue-and-red bird cuckooed five times.

The boy held up the note. "Should we show this to the police?"

"I think we better."

REFLECTIONS

POINT TO PONDER

Mrs. Alice told Isaac that troubles are the soil from which God grows His _____ warriors (brave men and women). Are you brave?

PEARL FROM GOD

"Praise the LORD, who is my rock. He trains my hands for war and gives my fingers skill for battle." (Psalm 144:1 NLT)

PRINCIPLE TO LIVE BY

Since the Garden of Eden, a war on earth has raged between good and evil. Therefore, beloved, be strong in the Lord. Know His good word, walk in His good ways, and courageously stand against evil.

Chapter 4:

Special Agents

Isaac copied the note before giving it to his dad that night. Mr. Fickle took it to Lou Carson the next morning. The deputy gave it to the sheriff. The sheriff handed it to FBI Special Agent Lee Wallace in charge of the missing-professor case.

"Who'd you say turned in this note, sheriff?" Wallace asked. "A pickle boy?"

"No, Fickle, with an F. Isaac Fickle."

Special Agent Wallace rubbed his chin. "Is that the same kid your deputies pulled out of the tunnel?"

"Yes, sir, one and the same, along with his brother, Jacob."

"Have Deputy Carson report to me. I have some questions about those two."

Wednesday, 4: 07 P.M.

"Thanks a lot, Fish Fry," Jacob spewed. "Now we're in trouble with the FBI."

Isaac's stomach tied in a thousand knots.

Mr. Fickle shook his head. "No, you're not in trouble. Lou said they just want to ask you some questions. Now, go get in the van, guys. We don't want to be late."

Jacob reached for the keys. "Can I drive?"

"Sure."

Mrs. Fickle hugged Isaac and whispered, "Everything'll be fine. You did the right thing."

On the ride to the Monroe County Sheriff's Department, Isaac remembered an old Swedish proverb Mrs. Alice had taught him: "Worry often gives a small thing a big shadow." He felt like a shadow deeper than Fall Creek Gorge loomed over him.

What if they don't believe us?

What if they think we had something to do with Professor Sparrow disappearing?

What if they arrest us and throw us in juvie?

What if . . .

Jacob interrupted the spiraling what-ifs. "You know, Dad, this is kinda cool — meetin' with the FBI."

"Quite the adventure! Keep your eyes on the road, bud, and turn left at the next light."

4:29 P.M.

Lou Carson met them at the door. "Well, if it isn't the infamous Fickle fugitives." He shook hands with Mr. Fickle. "How you doin', Stephen?"

"We're good, Lou. I think the boys here are a little nervous."

The deputy mussed Isaac's hair. "Nothing to be nervous about, son. We're the good guys. We want to find Sparrow safe and sound just as much as you do."

He led them down a hallway. *The walk of doom,* Isaac thought. A long trek to the principal's office as a fourth grader flashed in his mind. Big trucks carrying circus animals had passed by the school, and he along with half the class had run to the window to watch. The substitute teacher sent the whole bunch to Mrs. Adams's office. The principal told them to be kind and helpful because the sub was having a hard day. *That day turned out okay*, Isaac encouraged himself. *Maybe today will too*.

The deputy knocked on a door labeled "Special Operations."

A gruff voice boomed, "Come in."

"Agent Wallace, this is Stephen Fickle, and these are his sons, Jacob and Isaac."

The burly man behind a large desk piled with papers motioned to three chairs. "Have a seat, gentlemen."

Lou Carson turned to leave. "Deputy, I'd like you to stay," Agent Wallace ordered.

"Yes, sir." Deputy Carson closed the door.

Wallace pulled a white notepad from a drawer. "So, boys, what's your connection to Benjamin Sparrow?"

Jacob squirmed.

Isaac's face looked as white as Agent Wallace's notebook. The boy turned to his dad.

Mr. Fickle turned to Jacob. "So, Jacob, why don't you tell Agent Wallace how you met Professor Sparrow."

Jacob cleared his throat. "Well . . . uh . . . we used to think he was creepy."

"Kids said he put spiders in Halloween candy," Isaac added in a small voice, "but that wasn't true."

Lou Carson bit a cheek to keep from laughing.

"A couple of years ago," Jacob said, "I helped my friend, Mark Williams, solve Professor Sparrow's history mystery. That's how we found the tunnels."

Wallace made a note on the paper. "Tell me about those tunnels."

Jacob scooted to the edge of his seat. "It's a really cool story, sir. Professor Sparrow bought Asa Watts' house when he first moved to Indiana. Asa Watts was Mrs. Alice

— uh, Mrs. Alice Holtshausen's — great-great-grandfather. Anyway, Professor Sparrow found an awesome map in the attic that led him to the tunnels, and, for some reason, he decided not to tell anybody. Instead, he made up a riddle for his IU students and promised them an 'A' if they figured it out."

"Yeah, I've heard about that. Go on."

"Well, Mrs. Alice had Asa Watt's old journal. So, to make a long story short, Mark Williams, who was in Professor Sparrow's class at the time, and I . . ."

Wallace stopped him. "Why were you hanging out with a college guy?"

"'Cause he was my core group leader at church. Anyway, we put the entries from the old journal and Professor Sparrow's riddle together and found a trap door in the basement of our church. The door led to an underground triangle that connects the church and

Professor Sparrow's house and the old history building at IU."

Wallace scribbled on the pad. "Go on."

"The tunnels were hand-dug by members of Hebron Community Church before the Civil War. It took 'em three years! They stocked 'em with medical supplies and food and water and helped all kinds of people from the North and the South during the war."

"Hmm," Wallace muttered.

Wallace jotted.

"After we found the tunnels, Professor Sparrow invited us to his house, and we became friends. That's why I — uh, we — went in the tunnel that day. I thought Professor Sparrow might be down there hurt or something."

"How did you get in the house?"

"Professor Sparrow hid a key under a flowerpot and told me I could use it."

"Yes, sir, so it wasn't breaking and entering," Isaac interjected.

A chuckle slipped from Lou Carson.

"Are you still in contact with this Mark Williams guy?"

"Yes, sir. We're good friends. He's a junior now and the star of IU's track team. And he likes Mom's cooking, so he comes over to our house a lot. He ate supper with us last night."

"Hmm. So, where does this note come in?"

Jacob looked at Isaac. His younger brother rubbed sweaty palms on his jeans. "Well, sir, I went to Mrs. Alice's house, and she gave it to me."

"How did she get it?"

"Uh, she said Professor Sparrow gave it to her and told her to give it to us if there was trouble."

"Us?"

"Us boys, I guess — Mark or Jacob or me."

"When was the last time you saw Professor Sparrow?"

"Church," Isaac said.

Jacob nodded. "Yes, sir, at church, the Sunday before he disappeared."

"Any idea what this note means?"

"It means Professor Sparrow's in real trouble!" Jacob blurted. "And we need to find him fast."

"I think the note's a clue to *help* us find him," Isaac said.

"Hmm." Agent Wallace drummed his fingers on the chair arm and stared at Jacob and Isaac.

We're toast, Isaac thought. He watched the secondhand tick, tick, tick around the wall clock.

"Deputy Carson, do you believe these boys?"

"Yes, sir, I've known the Fickles for years. I trust every word to be true."

"Hmm."

Wallace drummed.

Wallace stared.

Wallace jotted.

Tick.

Tick.

Tick.

Agent Wallace leaned forward. "So, boys, how would you like to work for the FBI?"

REFLECTIONS

POINT TO PONDER

Agent Wallace asked Jacob and Isaac to _____ for the FBI. Has anyone ever asked for your help with a big job? What was the job? What did you do?

PEARL FROM GOD

"Therefore, we are Christ's ambassadors; God is making His appeal through us. " *(2 Corinthians 5:20 NLT)*

PRINCIPLE TO LIVE BY

Agent Wallace recruited Jacob and Isaac to work for him. God has appointed us, beloved, to work for Him as His ambassadors (His representatives or special agents). It is Christ's plan to make His appeal to lost people through us, begging them to be reconciled to God. Agent _____ (your name), your assignment, should you choose to accept it: Go tell the world about Jesus!

Chapter 5:

Game On

"Agent Wallace, if you don't mind my asking, why in the Sam Hill would you enlist a couple of kids as 'Special Agents' (Deputy Carson made quotation marks with his fingers) for the FBI? Uh, sir."

"Call it a hunch, but I think those two are a major key to finding Sparrow." Wallace held up the note. "Obviously, the old man trusted their intuition."

Working for the FBI felt like a reality video game: Decode the note, find the missing professor, and race to the finish line. Team Jacob vs Team Isaac. Who will win? The sixteen-year-old and his rowdy friends? Or a sixth grader and a granny? Game on!

3:44 P.M.

Team Jacob

After school on Friday, Lou Carson pointed a flashlight down the old shaft. "So, where does this go?"

"Hebron Community Church," Jacob told him.

"To a trap door in the basement, right?" Deputy Carson asked.

"Yes, sir. Under the old altar."

Mark Williams pointed to the second shaft. "And that's the northwest tunnel. It runs 4,657 feet to the old history building at IU."

Deputy Carson shook his head. "Amazing."

"And there's a third tunnel connecting the history building back to the church — a two-and-a-half-mile triangle," Jacob explained. "So, if we split up, we could cover ground faster and meet halfway around."

"No can do. We're sticking together," Deputy Carson said. "Wallace's orders. That's the only way he let you guys down here."

"Yes, sir."

Wallace thumped a timber. "It this thing safe?"

Mark nodded. "Yes, sir. Indiana declared it a historical landmark. So, all the rotten timbers were replaced to make it safe for the Archeology Department to dig for artifacts."

"Okay, then. Which way?"

Mark pointed left. "Northwest tunnel. Professor Sparrow used it for years as a shortcut from his house to the history building."

Team Isaac

"Hop in!" Mrs. Alice called from Gertie's driver's seat.

"Where we going?" Isaac asked.

"Ben Sparrow's house."

"But Jacob and Mark and Deputy Carson are over there."

"They're in the tunnels. We'll be outside."

"I gotta ask my Mom."

"Called her before I came."

Mrs. Fickle stepped out the front door and waved. "Hi, Mrs. Alice."

"Hey, sugar. Thanks for letting me borrow your boy."

Elizabeth hopped off the rope swing hanging from a high limb. "I wanna go!"

"Sure, honey, jump on in. The more the merrier."

"You guys have fun," Mrs. Fickle called. "And behave!"

Elizabeth crawled to the backseat. Isaac plopped down on the cracked-leather passenger seat and closed the heavy door.

"Buckle up, children. Gertie likes to scoot!"

Seatbelts clicked.

Gertie shot out of the driveway like a cannonball — backwards.

A horn blared.

Tires squealed.

Isaac ducked.

Elizabeth giggled.

"Crazy drivers," Mrs. Alice muttered and floored it down Mulberry Street. She peered through the steering wheel at everything but the road. "Look how tall the grass has grown in the cemetery. I'll call Reverend Wheeler this evening and let him know."

Gertie's right tires slid to the shoulder, spraying gravel like a sprinkler. Mrs. Alice whipped back on the pavement and barreled through the stop sign at Church Street and Rabbit Road. Elizabeth cackled. Isaac gripped the door handle. White-knuckled. *I'm gonna die!* he thought. He hadn't felt this scared since the Fourth of July as a toddler. The deafening fireworks had traumatized the baby for years. Anything "youd" freaked him out.

Team Jacob

"Stop." Deputy Carson held up his hand. "Cut the lights. I hear something."

Voices drifted through the darkness.

"Somebody's down here," Jacob whispered.

"You boys wait here." Lou Carson worked his way down the black passageway.

Step.

By step.

Inch.

By inch.

The voices grew louder.

Footsteps pounded damp clay.

A speck of light moved up the tunnel.

Carson edged closer.

Forty yards.

Mark and Jacob held their breath.

Thirty yards.

Twenty.

Ten.

"Freeze!" Deputy Carson yelled and hit the spotlight.

Something clanked. Two giant shadows turned and hightailed it down the northwest tunnel. Carson followed in hot pursuit.

"Come on!" Jacob yelled.

Jacob zoomed past Deputy Carson. Mark passed them both, soaring toward the history building.

Pound.

Pound.

Pound.

Up ahead, light poured through the open trap door. Jacob saw hulky suspects scrambling up slippery, wooden steps with Mark on their heels.

Team Isaac

Gertie screeched to a halt, mere inches from Deputy Carson's patrol car parked at Professor Sparrow's front gates.

Mrs. Alice smiled. "Here we are, children."

I'm alive! Isaac refrained from jumping out and kissing the ground.

Mrs. Alice shuffled toward the iron gates and shook each one with boney hands. Next, she circled the stone pillars and jabbed them with her cane.

Elizabeth whispered, "What's she doin'?"

Isaac shrugged. "Uh, Mrs. Alice, whatcha doing?"

"Looking."

"For what?" Elizabeth asked.

"Another clue. The note said *watching for me daily at my gates.* Maybe Ben left something down here for you children to find."

"Good thinking!" Elizabeth said and kicked at leaves on the ground.

Mrs. Alice poked along the fence.

Isaac shook the gates again. "Find anything?" he asked.

"Not yet," Mrs. Alice said.

Shiny blue under brown leaves caught Elizabeth's eye. She picked up a piece of broken glass. *Ooh, this is pretty,* she thought. *And here's another one and another and another! These are perfect for my art project.* She zipped the treasures into her jacket pocket.

"I'll check up here," Isaac called.

"Ok," Mrs. Alice said. "Keep an eye out for clues."

Isaac raced up the driveway. Athleticism and speed were two of his strong suits. By two, he could dribble a basketball. By six, soccer coaches were calling him "Wheels." Last summer, he made the 1000-Club for soccer ball juggling.

The boy stopped halfway up the hill. A breeze rattled the treetops. An eerie feeling that someone was watching him rattled Isaac. He looked toward the house. On the front porch, a stranger crouched in the shadows!

Team Jacob

Crimson hoodies disappeared through the hole. The trap door banged shut.

BUMP.

SCRAPE.

THUD.

Mark pushed hard against the door. It wouldn't budge.

Jacob panted behind him. "Did you . . . see . . . their faces?"

Mark shook his head.

Deputy Carson trotted up, breathing heavily. "Any . . . other way . . . into the building . . . from here?"

"No . . . sir," Jacob gasped. "What . . . do we . . . do now?"

Deputy Carson motioned. "Come on . . . let's see . . . what they dropped."

Team Isaac

"Mrs. Alice!" Isaac flew back down the hill. "Mrs. Alice! Somebody's on the front porch!"

She squinted toward the house. "Hey, you up there! Come on out here where we can see you."

Isaac wanted to disappear.

The stranger did.

Team Jacob

Deputy Carson's flashlight found two shovels and a canvas bag. "Don't touch anything. Fingerprints."

"Hey, over here." Jacob pointed to a red plastic rectangle on the tunnel floor.

"Don't touch it."

"Yes, sir."

Mark squatted for a better look. "Hoosier meal card, and there's a name on it."

Deputy Carson shot a thumbs up. "Good work, gentlemen."

REFLECTIONS

POINT TO PONDER

Jacob and Isaac are in a _____ to decode the note and find Professor Sparrow. What goals are you racing toward in your life? Who are you running with to accomplish your goals?

PEARL FROM GOD

"Run from anything that stimulates youthful lusts. Instead, pursue righteous living, faithfulness, love, and peace. Enjoy the companionship of those who call on the Lord with pure hearts." (2 Timothy 2:22 NLT)

PRINCIPLE TO LIVE BY

In his letter to Timothy, the Apostle Paul told his young friend to run away from sin, to run toward righteousness, faith, love, and peace, and to run with people who are seeking the Lord with pure hearts. Beloved, I encourage you to do the same!

Chapter 6:

Shadows

10:16 P.M.

Isaac tossed and turned on the top bunk that was Jacob's before he moved downstairs to his own room. Pieces to the missing-professor puzzle swarmed his brain like seventeen-year cicadas.

Mysterious note.

Listen to me.

Watch at my gates.

Wait by my house.

Find me.

Find life.

Suspects in the tunnel.

Stranger on the porch.

Buzz.

Buzz.

Buzz.

Earlier, he had overheard Jacob and Mark talking about chasing two big guys in maroon hoodies through the tunnel. Isaac and Elizabeth agreed not to tell Jacob about the stranger — a strategy for winning the race.

A low moon spun shadowy webs on the floor. Isaac remembered the night he and Jacob first visited Professor Sparrow's. They were camping in the backyard when Dustin Harper had dared them to sneak over to the creepy, old mansion after dark. Professor Sparrow heard them and hit the flood lights. The boys hightailed it down Rabbit Road like a bear was on their heels — scared silly.

Isaac grinned at the memory. *Fear's like a dark shadow*, he thought, *it follows you around everywhere you go*. He turned toward the wall and whispered lines from

"When Evening Shadows Fall," a poem by James Whitcomb Riley he had learned at school:

"When evening shadows fall,

She hangs her cares away

Like empty garments on the wall

That hides her from the day;

And while old memories throng,

And vanished voices call,

She lifts her grateful heart in song

When evening shadows fall."

Hey, Professor Sparrow used lyrics in the history riddle, Isaac thought. *Maybe the words in the note are from a poem or song.*

"Her weary hands forget

The burdens of the day."

68

He yawned.

"The weight of sorrow and regret

In music rolls away . . ."

Sounds of steady breathing rose and fell from the top bunk. In the adjacent bedroom, Elizabeth danced over moon shadows, dreaming of the Irish Dancing World Championships in a land far away from suspects and strangers.

Moonlight spilled through lace curtains at the cottage with the peeling picket fence. Mrs. Alice sat in a Bentwood rocker, gazing at the silver globe in the night sky. "What a wondrous work of Your hands, Lord!" she whispered.

A Bible opened to Psalm 91 spread across her knees. She read, *"He that dwelleth in the secret place of the Most*

High shall abide under the shadow of the Almighty. I will say of the Lord, He is my refuge and my fortress; my God, in Him will I trust. His truth shall be thy shield and buckler. Thou shalt not be afraid."

Earlier, when Mrs. Alice brought the children home, Elizabeth had hopped straight from the car; Isaac lingered.

"What's on your mind, child?"

"Mrs. Alice, who do you think that was on Professor Sparrow's porch? And why did he run off so fast?"

"I suspect it was someone up to no good. Innocent folks don't flee. *'The wicked run when no one is chasing them, but an honest person is as brave as a lion.'"*

"Proverbs?" Isaac said.

"That's right. Proverbs 28:1. Good job!"

"I wish I was brave like a lion," Isaac muttered.

"Oh, you're braver than you think, child. It took courage for you to come over to my house and ask for help. Nelson Mandela once said . . . "

"Who's that?"

"Haven't you studied Nelson Mandela in school?"

Isaac shook his head.

"He was the President of South Africa in the 1990s."

"When my mom was my age, she wanted to be a missionary in Africa."

"Really? I didn't know that." Mrs. Alice pictured Rebekah Fickle sitting on the dirt floor of a grass hut teaching a circle of little children about Jesus. She smiled. "Now, what was I saying?"

"Nelson Mandela," Isaac reminded her.

"Oh, yes, Nelson Mandela. Like I was saying, President Mandela once said, *'I learned that courage was not the absence of fear, but the triumph over it. The brave man is not he who does not feel afraid, but he who conquers that fear.'"*

"What does that mean?"

"It means we all feel afraid at times, but we can't let fear win — paralyzing us to the point of becoming useless to the Lord."

Isaac frowned. "I don't wanna be useless."

"Of course, you don't. Neither do I. But with God's help, we can learn to conquer fear. Look!" Mrs. Alice pointed to the birdfeeder in the maple tree. "A rose-breasted grosbeak. The first one I've seen this fall."

"How?"

Mrs. Alice looked bewildered. "How what, dear?"

"How can we conquer fear?" Isaac asked.

"Trust God."

The boy sighed. "You make it sound so easy."

"It's not easy, but it is simple. When we don't trust God, we feel afraid. When we do trust Him, we don't. After my J. W. died, I felt scared every night in that old house all by myself. I finally got fed up with living that way and talked to God about it. You know what He said?"

"What?"

"God reminded me that I'm never really alone. He's always with me, and I can trust Him. So, I decided right then and there to stop being a scaredy cat and trust God, even when it's dark outside."

"Did it work?'

"Well, I still feel afraid at times, but when I do, I remember that God is with me, and He gives me courage. And the more I remember, the less fear I feel."

Isaac's face grew serious. "I hope I can remember that."

"I'm going to pray that every time you're afraid, Isaac, you remember God is with you, and you find courage."

"Thank you, Mrs. Alice."

"You are most welcome, Isaac."

The boy opened the car door to leave.

"And one more thing," Mrs. Alice said.

"What's that?"

"Sing."

His face scrunched up like a prune. "Sing?"

"Yes, sing to the Lord, and He'll strengthen your heart." When Mrs. Alice said heart, both arms flew up, honking the horn.

She grinned. "See! Gertie agrees."

Isaac laughed.

Outside her window, a breeze swayed tree branches. Mrs. Alice stared at the winking moon. "Thank You, Lord, for keeping me company. I'd be lost without You." She chuckled. "Eternally lost. Please be with Ben tonight. Keep him safe under the shadow of Your wing. And Lord, give Isaac courage. Help that boy trust You and overcome his fears."

Morton rubbed against Mrs. Alice's housecoat. She stroked his back. "Hey, pretty boy. So, what does Ben's note mean? Hmm?"

Meow.

"Ben, what are you trying to tell the boys through those cryptic verses?"

Meow.

Mrs. Alice snapped her fingers. Morton jumped. "Verses! That's it!"

Blocks away, a shadow crossed Professor Sparrow's backyard. Snatching the key from under the flowerpot, the figure unlocked the backdoor and slipped inside.

REFLECTONS

POINT TO PONDER

Isaac compared _____ to a dark shadow. What are you afraid of?

PEARL FROM GOD

"On my bed I remember You; I think of You through the watches of the night. Because You are my help, I sing in the shadow of Your wings. I cling to You; Your right hand upholds me." (Psalm 63:6-8)

PRINCIPLE TO LIVE BY

A shadow is a dark shape made by on object coming between light rays and a surface. To abide in God's shadow means staying close to Him with God standing between you and evil. That's not to say that bad things will never happen, beloved. Undoubtedly, they will. However, God will be with you and uphold you when they do!

Chapter 7:

Together

Saturday, 8:37 A.M.

Mr. Fickle stuck a dirty glass in the dishwasher. "Enough of this competing against each other business," he said. "A house divided can't stand. We need to do something to reunite this family."

Mrs. Fickle wiped splattered bacon grease from the stove top and rinsed the sponge under the faucet. "I agree. How about a picnic and hike after Elizabeth's Irish-step-dance class today?"

Mr. Fickle grinned. "Perfect!"

Jacob poked his head in the kitchen. "Can I drive?"

Jacob parked the minivan and shut off the ignition. "Not too crowded, today," he said. "Only two other cars."

"Three." Isaac pointed to a white, Chevy pickup truck pulling into the far end of the parking lot.

"That looks like Grandpa Willowkins' farm truck," Elizabeth said.

"Okay, kids, let's go," Mr. Fickle said.

Five Fickles marched down a trail in Cedar Bluffs Nature Preserve. A crystal creek splashed beside the path. Gnarled cedars clung to neighboring cliffs. A familiar friend darted under a split-rail fence and joined the hike.

"Stella!" Elizabeth shouted.

The black and white Australian shepherd lived near the park. Her tag read: "If you find me in Cedar Bluffs Preserve, please leave me. I have a home, am loved, and well cared for."

"Get it, Stella!" Isaac hurled a stick into the rushing water.

Playing fetch was a favorite game. The dog dove in and leaped out with the prize.

Arf, arf!

"Good girl!" Isaac said and scrubbed her head.

Fall colors painted the woods. Squirrels chased through the treetops. Rocks and uneven terrain scarred the trail leading to the foot of high bluffs. A narrow path under golden-bronze and scarlet oaks led to the pinnacle.

"Today's a great day!" Isaac said.

The boy loved family hikes. Their hardest adventure had been a steep climb to Charlie's Bunion last March on the Appalachian Trail in the Great Smoky Mountains of Tennessee. The scariest hike he could remember was Brough's Folly in Clifty Falls, an old railroad tunnel that burrowed so deep into the hillside that it turned pitch-black. He thought they were lost forever and going to die. Phones provided enough light to pick their way through the spooky, bat-filled passage. A sign at the other end read: Do Not Enter This Tunnel.

"Stay on the trail," Mr. Fickle instructed, "and don't get in a hurry. It's slippery in spots."

Stella led the charge up the hill. Jacob followed. Then Isaac. Next came Elizabeth and Mrs. Fickle with Mr. Fickle as the rearguard.

Near the top, Isaac's tennis shoe slipped on wet moss. He pitched backwards. Elizabeth caught him. "Whoa, dude, you nearly knocked us down the hill like dominoes."

"Sorry."

"It's okay. Just watch your step."

He hurried to catch up with Jacob. "Hey, Jacob, do you get the feeling somebody's following us?"

Jacob laughed. "Duh. It's a hiking trail, Fish Fry. Of course, somebody's following us. They're ahead of us, too."

"I know, but I just have that funny feeling again."

"Whatcha mean *again*?"

"Uh . . . nothing. It's probably nothing."

When they reached the pinnacle, the family perched on the rocky ledge. Southern Indiana spread below in all her glory.

"That was fun," Isaac said.

"Yeah," Jacob agreed. "It's one of my favorite trails."

"So, what made it fun for you, Isaac?" Mr. Fickle asked.

"Well, it wasn't easy, but we did it! A guy at school came out here with his family, but they turned back before they got to the top."

"Would you try this hike by yourself?" Mr. Fickle asked.

"No, 'cause you wouldn't let us," Elizabeth piped.

Everybody laughed.

"If you had *permission*, would you make the hike alone?"

"Probably," Jacob said.

Isaac shook his head. "I don't know. It might be a little spooky out here by myself, and I'm glad Elizabeth was there to catch me when I slipped."

"That reminds me of a Bible verse," Mrs. Fickle said. *"Two people are better off than one. If one person falls, the other can reach out and help. But someone who falls alone is in real trouble."*

Isaac grinned. "That's cool, Mom. Where's that verse?"

"Old Testament, Ecclesiastes 4:9-10."

"So, how's the hunt for Professor Sparrow going?" Mr. Fickle asked.

"Fine," Jacob said.

Isaac nodded. "Good."

"Anything new?" Mrs. Fickle asked.

Jacob brushed mud from his jeans. Isaac picked moss from the rock. Neither spoke a word.

"Well, if you count Jacob chasing two big guys through the tunnel, and Isaac seeing a stranger on

Professor Sparrow's front porch," Elizabeth blurted, "I'd say some new things are happening."

"Elizabeth!" Isaac yelled.

"Well, it's true."

"Jacob Fickle, what's this about you chasing guys through the tunnel?" Mrs. Fickle cried.

"It's okay, Mom. Deputy Carson was with me. And Mark Williams, too. Anyway, how'd you know, Elizabeth?"

"Haven't you heard? I'm on Team Isaac now. He overheard you talking to Mark."

"You weren't supposed to tell!" Isaac hollered. "You promised."

"Sorry."

Jacob snapped, "That's not fair! Why didn't you tell me about the stranger, Fish Fry?"

"'Cause . . . "

"Guys, guys," Mr. Fickle interrupted. "I think we've lost focus here. This is *not* a game. We have a friend who is missing. Professor Sparrow may be in serious trouble, and the FBI believes our family can help find him. From now on, there are no *teams*. Understood?"

"Yes, sir."

"The Bible teaches working *together*. That means seeking God together, sharing information, and doing everything we can to help our friend — together."

"Yes, sir."

Mr. Fickle looked his children in the eye. "The world may define success as a dog-eat-dog fight to the top — no offense, Stella — but God's ways are not the world's ways. The measure of a successful man in God's eyes is to walk humbly with the Lord and treat others with respect and kindness."

"Yes, sir."

Mrs. Fickle's phone buzzed. "It's Mrs. Alice . . . Hey, Mrs. Alice."

(pause)

"Oh, just sittin' on top of a cliff."

(pause)

"Yes, ma'am, we can do that. See you in a little while."

(pause)

"Love you, too. Bye now."

"What'd she say?" Isaac asked.

"She asked us to come by on the way home. She said she's figured out what the note means."

On the trail back to the parking lot, Isaac glimpsed something or someone ducking into the woods. *Probably just a squirrel,* he convinced himself and forced his mind in a different direction.

If Mrs. Alice cracked the note, then Professor Sparrow could be home by suppertime . . . or headed to Peaceful Rest Funeral Home. Imaginations of a tombstone inscribed "Here lies Professor Benjamin Sparrow" made him shudder. He dropped the awful thought and called, "Hey, Jacob, wait for me!"

REFLECTIONS

POINT TO PONDER

The Bible teaches that together is better than _____.

Who do you like working with? Why?

PEARL FROM GOD

"What are you really accomplishing here? Why are you trying to do all this alone . . . This is not good . . . You're going to wear yourself out . . . This job is too heavy a burden for you to handle all by yourself . . . select from all the people some capable, honest men who fear God . . . They will help you carry the load, making the task easier for you." (Exodus 18:14-22 NLT)

PRINCIPLE TO LIVE BY

In the Bible, the Church is likened to a body. Jesus is the head. Believers are the many parts, all working together to accomplish God's purposes. Life is not a competition, beloved. It's a community — a community created to help one another, to tell the world about Jesus, and to bring God glory!

Chapter 8:

Puzzle Piece

4:23 P.M.

Mrs. Alice was on the porch grinning when Jacob turned the van onto the driveway. She tottered down the steps.

Mrs. Fickle hugged her. "Where's your cane, Mrs. Alice?"

"Oh, mercy. I got so excited I completely forgot about it."

Mr. Fickle rubbed white flecks from the picket fence and made a mental note: *run to Menards for paint next week.*

"Where in the world were you, sugar?" Mrs. Alice asked. "On top of a cliff?"

Mrs. Fickle laughed. "Cedar Bluffs Nature Preserve."

"It's so beautiful out there. My J.W. and I used to take the children on those trails. Such happy memories. Well, come in, come in. Are you thirsty? I made lemonade and a batch of my mother's delicious shortbread cookies."

"That sounds amazing," Mr. Fickle said.

Isaac held Mrs. Alice's arm as they climbed the steps. "Mom said you figured out the note?"

She patted his cheek. "Patience, child. Patience."

A china plate of warm cookies and pitcher of fresh-squeezed lemonade sat on the kitchen table.

"Sit down, everybody."

"May we wash our hands first?" Mrs. Fickle asked.

"Certainly. The powder room's right down the hall."

The quaint bathroom smelled of English lavender. A white towel crocheted in pink hung by the porcelain basin, and an old-fashioned clawfoot tub sat in one corner.

Mrs. Fickle took a deep breath. "It smells like my grandmother's house."

Jacob grabbed a handful of cookies.

"Just two," Mrs. Fickle said.

"He's a growing boy, Rebekah. Let that child have all he wants." Mrs. Alice smiled. "My, it's wonderful to have folks around the table again."

Isaac stuffed a cookie in his mouth and mumbled. "Peppermint and Butterscotch."

"Where?" Elizabeth looked for candy.

"Out there." He pointed to the birdfeeder. "And if you see a yellow finch, that's Lemon Drop."

"For real?" Elizabeth asked. "There's a blue jay. What's his name?"

"He doesn't have a name yet," Mrs. Alice said. "Why don't you name him, Elizabeth?"

"Azure."

Jacob wrinkled his nose. "Azure? What kind of name is that?"

"Azure is bright, cyan-blue named after the mineral azurite. I learned that in art class at school."

"Then Azure it is," Mrs. Alice said.

"Mrs. Alice, what about the note?" Isaac asked.

She pretended not to hear. "Does anyone need more lemonade?"

"No, ma'am, we're filled to the gills. But everything was so delicious," Mrs. Fickle said.

"Then let's move to the parlor. I have something to show you."

"Finally," Isaac said under his breath.

Elizabeth sat down on the green velvet loveseat. Morton jumped in her lap. "Aww. Are you lonesome?" She stroked his back. "Do you miss Professor Sparrow? I'm sure he misses you, too."

On a rainy, summer night nine years back, the professor had heard pitiful meowing and discovered a black and gray kitten hunkered on his windowsill, soaked to the bone. The old man took him in, named him Morton after Oliver P. Morton the fourteenth Governor of Indiana during the American Civil War, and, as they say, the rest is history.

Mrs. Alice opened a huge King James Bible on the coffee table. "Does this sound familiar?" She read, *"Blessed is the man that heareth me, watching daily at my gates, waiting at the posts of my doors. For whoso findeth me findeth life and shall obtain favour of the LORD.* Proverbs 8:34-35."

"The note!" Isaac cried. "Sorta."

Mr. Fickle had his cell phone out scrolling. "That's the King James version. According to this, Professor Sparrow's note was written in the New Living Translation. '*Joyful are those who listen to me, watching for me daily at my gates, waiting for me outside my home. For whoever finds me finds life.*'"

Jacob looked confused. "But why would Professor Sparrow give us a Bible verse?"

"Yeah," Isaac said. "And who is 'me' in those verses?"

"Good question," Mr. Fickle said.

Mrs. Alice turned the Bible toward the boy. "Here, Isaac, read verses one and twelve."

"Verse one says: *Listen as wisdom calls out*, and verse twelve says*: I, wisdom, live together with good judgment."* His hopes fell. "That doesn't tell us where Professor Sparrow is."

"No, but it gives us the next piece of the puzzle," Jacob said. "Joyful are those who listen to *wisdom*, watching for *wisdom* daily at my gates, waiting for *wisdom* outside my home! For whoever finds *wisdom* finds life."

Isaac jumped to his feet. "Then what are we waitin' for? Let's go find wisdom!"

Outside, a white Chevy truck slowly rolled by the cottage with the peeling picket fence.

REFLECTIONS

POINT TO PONDER

Professor Sparrow's note contained Scripture verses from

the _____. How often do you read the Bible?

PEARL FROM GOD

"*All Scripture is God-breathed and is useful for teaching,*

rebuking, correcting and training in righteousness, so that the

servant of God may be thoroughly equipped for every good

work." (*2 Timothy 3:16*)

PRINCIPLE TO LIVE BY

The Bible is the living word of God, His instruction book for

life. Read it, beloved. Think about God's words and obey

them. If you do, your life will be better and so will you!

Chapter 9:

Strongbox

Tuesday, 3:48 P.M.

"Name?" Agent Wallace growled.

"Sam . . . uh, Samuel J. Westinghouse, sir."

"Age?"

"Nineteen. Am I in trouble?"

Agent Wallace scribbled on a notepad. "Depends. Why were you in the tunnel?"

Sam gripped the edges of the seat. "Do I need a lawyer?"

"Depends. Answer my question, son. Why were you down in the tunnel?"

Sam's size 13 tennis shoe tapped the floor nervously. "Uh . . . 'cause I'm stupid?"

Deputy Carson chuckled. Agent Wallace frowned. "Tell me something I don't already know, kid. Why were you down there?"

"I can't lose my scholarship."

"Then you better start talking. Why were you in that tunnel?"

Earlier that afternoon, Sam Westinghouse was at IU football practice when a sheriff's car parked outside Memorial Stadium. Two deputies marched on the field and handed a paper to the offensive-line coach.

"Westinghouse," the coach yelled, "go with these men."

Sam pulled off his helmet. "Now?"

"Now! You, too, Morgan."

"Okay, so last week, this guy came up to us after class . . . "

"What class?"

"History. I'm in Professor Sparrow's . . . well, not anymore. I'm in some grad student's American History class."

"Us?"

"Sir?"

"You said some guy came up to *us*? Who is *us*?"

"Oh, just some of my football buddies. Anyway, this guy comes up and says, 'Who wants to make a quick hundred bucks?' I'm thinking the dude's a drug dealer or something, but he says all we have to do is dig a hole and find something he buried."

Scribble.

Scribble.

"Go on."

"What college student says no to a hundred bucks, right? Uh, when it's not illegal or anything."

Scribble.

"Okay . . . so, me and my buddy, Shawn, said, 'Sure! We'll do it,' and he told us to meet him in the basement of the history building at 4:00 o'clock Friday afternoon. So, we did."

"What did the guy look like?"

"Kinda old. Maybe 'bout your age."

Deputy Carson coughed to smother a laugh.

"Details. I want details. White? Black? Hispanic? Asian?"

"White."

"Tall, short?"

"Uh, kinda tall, but not as tall as me."

"Hair?"

"Yes, sir. He had hair."

Agent Wallace rolled his eyes. "Hair *color*?"

"Brown with some gray here and here." Sam touched his temples. "And a mustache. Just a regular looking guy."

"So, what were you supposed to be looking for?"

"A strongbox."

"And where were you supposed to dig?"

"Northwest tunnel. He had this map-looking thing of the tunnels and told us to walk 2,400 feet down the northwest tunnel."

"So, let me get this straight. A guy you've never seen before promises you a hundred bucks to go dig in a tunnel that's closed to the public?"

"Yes, sir, but he said he had permission from the Archeology Department."

"And you believed him?"

"Yes, sir."

Agent Wallace shook his head. "Go on."

"Then, he looked at my feet and asked if I could count."

Both Carson and Wallace laughed out loud.

"I said, 'Yes, sir,' and he said to walk 552 paces and dig there. Then he made me repeat it back to him."

"Why did you run when Deputy Carson told you to stop?"

"I didn't want to get in trouble. I can't lose my scholarship."

"You said that already. Okay, Westinghouse. That's all for now. Deputy Carson, bring in Shawn Morgan. Oh, one more thing. What was the guy's name?"

Sam shrugged. "He didn't say. I didn't ask."

"Okay, you can go." Agent Wallace pulled something out of the desk drawer. "And here's your meal card."

"Thanks."

Sam gave Shawn a fist bump as he walked out and his teammate walked in.

REFLECTIONS

POINT TO PONDER

A stranger paid Sam Westinghouse to look for a

_____. What do you think might be

hidden in that strongbox?

PEARL FROM GOD

"The LORD is my rock, my fortress, and my savior; my God is my rock, in whom I find protection. He is my shield and the horn of my salvation, my stronghold." (Psalm 18:2)

PRINCIPLE TO LIVE BY

A strongbox is a metal chest used to safeguard valuables from fire and theft. Beloved, when you trust in the work of Lord Jesus on the cross, God is your strongbox — your place of eternal safety. Seek Him with all your heart!

Chapter 10:

Let Us Pray

Wednesday, 3:55 P.M.

Twelve days had passed since Benjamin Sparrow disappeared. Hopes of finding the professor alive and well were fading like the floral paper on his kitchen walls. The team of deputies Agent Wallace ordered 552 paces down the northwest tunnel came back empty-handed. No strongbox. No new clues. When Agent Wallace heard the boys' speculated meaning of the note, he grunted, "Wisdom? That's it? Is the old guy a few cogs short of a clock?"

7:03 P.M.

Church members, friends of Professor Sparrow, IU students, and curious reporters packed the pews of the prayer service at Hebron Community Church. Mrs. Alice and Isaac shared a hymnal and sang with gusto, "I once was lost but now I'm found, was blind but now I see."

Reverend Wheeler stepped to the pulpit. "Dearly beloved, we are gathered here tonight on behalf of our brother, Benjamin Sparrow. Let us approach God's throne with confidence and find grace to help in this hour of need. Nothing is impossible for the Lord Most High, and our trust is in Him."

"Amen," a loud voice boomed from the back pew.

"I've asked Alice Hotzhausen to start us off tonight. Mrs. Alice."

Mrs. Alice hobbled down the aisle. Her thoughts rewound to June 1957. Alice Ann McCarthy, carrying a nosegay of blue hydrangeas and lilies of the valley from her mother's garden, walked that same aisle. A full, white-satin skirt emphasized her tiny waist. Green eyes sparkled behind the long, net veil as she promised God and J.W., "Till death do us part, I pledge thee my faith and love." *My, he was handsome in that black suit,* she thought.

Reverend Wheeler helped her up the steps to the pulpit. "Are you ready, Mrs. Alice?"

"Yes. Thank you, Reverend," she said. "Let us pray."

Heads bowed.

"Dear Heavenly Father, thank You for hearing our prayers tonight for Ben Sparrow. Protect him, Lord, and guide those searching for him. Give them courage and wisdom and competence. And Lord, if someone has intended him harm, please turn his heart toward you and save him by Your grace. In Jesus' name we pray, Amen."

"Amen," the congregation echoed.

The pastor stepped back to the mic. "Thank you, Mrs. Alice. Mark Williams, a student at IU and close friend of Professor Sparrow, will now pray. Mark."

Mark helped Mrs. Alice to her seat and then hurried up the platform. "Thank you, Reverend Wheeler," he said. "Before I pray, I'd like to thank you guys for coming tonight. Jesus said in Matthew 18:20 where two or three are gathered in His name, He's there also. Let us pray. Lord Jesus, thank You for Your presence here tonight. Please watch over Professor Sparrow wherever he is. Help us understand the clues he left behind and guide our steps to our missing friend. In Jesus' name. Amen."

"Amen."

Mr. Fickle, Lou Carson, the chairmen of the deacons, and Reverend Wheeler each prayed in turn. Isaac's eyes roamed from the worn carpet under his orange tennis shoes to the chandelier above his head and eventually landed on the gold cross behind the altar. *Lord, he silently prayed, why do You say yes to some prayers and no to others? Please, please, please say yes to our prayers tonight.*

The congregation rose to their feet and crooned Fanny Crosby's "He Hideth My Soul." No one noticed the stranger from Professor Sparrow's front porch slip from the back pew and disappear into the night.

REFLECTIONS

POINT TO PONDER

Hebron Community Church gathered people to _____ for Professor Sparrow. What are you asking God for?

PEARL FROM GOD

"Devote yourselves to prayer with an alert mind and a thankful heart." (Colossians 4:2)

PRINCIPLE TO LIVE BY

Simply put, prayer is talking to God. Throughout the Bible, God invites us over and over and over again to pray — to talk to Him. Beloved, pray first. Pray often. Pray to Jesus and never give up!

Chapter 11:

Message in a Bottle

Thursday, 3:41 P.M.

Elizabeth arranged blue glass slivers over a poster

board and stepped back for a better look.

"Whatcha doing?" Isaac asked.

"Art project."

He cocked his head sideways. "What's it supposed to be?"

"It's not *supposed* to be anything. It *is* TREASURED TRASH."

Isaac wrinkled his nose. "If you say so."

"We had to draw a quote out of sack," Elizabeth explained, "and then make something to symbolize its meaning."

"What'd you pick?"

"One man's trash is another man's treasure. Get it? TREASURED TRASH."

He nodded. "I get it."

Isaac and Elizabeth Fickle were polar opposites. He viewed life literally and mathematically. His sister, on the other hand, beheld the universe through the fanciful lens of art, literature, dance, and music. Isaac took piano lessons because he had to; Elizabeth because she loved to. She had once tried luring her little brother into Mozart. "It's math and speed all in one!" she coaxed, but Isaac didn't take the bait.

"Where'd you get the broken glass?" Isaac asked.

"Professor Sparrow's."

"The day we saw the stranger?"

"Mm-hmm." She rearranged pieces for the third time. "I love this shade of cobalt blue."

Isaac studied the posterboard. "Scoot 'em together."

"Why?"

"'Cause, look." He pointed. "There are letters in the glass."

"Letters? Whatcha mean letters? I don't see any letters."

114

"Just push 'em together . . . Now, turn that one around . . . Yeah, and move that piece to the other side."

Elizabeth gasped. "Oh, my goodness!"

"Mom!" Isaac yelled. "You gotta come see this! Hurry!"

Mrs. Fickle clicked the search bar on the family computer and typed in the words formed into the glass: "J. Wise, Allentown, PA." An image of a blue bottle popped up.

"Here it is!" she said. "And listen to this. Civil-War era cobalt blue glass blob-top soda bottles were fabricated for Pennsylvania bottler James Wise. These historical artifacts are commonly found in privy digs."

"What's a privy dig?" Isaac asked.

"It's when antique and bottle collectors dig up the contents of old outhouses."

Isaac made a face. "Ooh, nasty."

Mrs. Fickle laughed. "Only the ones that haven't been used in a blue moon. Look at the picture."

Jacob, Elizabeth, and Isaac crowded around the computer screen.

"Perfect match," Jacob said. "It's all starting to come together. So, Professor Sparrow tells us in the note to watch for *wisdom* at the gates of his house built before the Civil War. And Elizabeth finds a broken bottle near the gates made during the Civil War by some guy named *Wise* in Allentown, Pennsylvania. Let's go look for more glass."

Mrs. Fickle raised a hand. "Hold on, Jacob. The first thing we need to do is call Lou Carson and tell him what you've found."

"I'll call," Isaac said and picked up his mom's cell phone.

Jacob grabbed the phone. "No, Fish Fry, I'm gonna call."

116

"Hey, give that back!" Isaac hollered. "I'm the one who figured out the glass spelled something."

Elizabeth pointed a finger at herself. "Well, I'm the one who found the glass."

Mrs. Fickle pointed to the kitchen. "Get the fishbowl. The name I draw calls."

Friday, 10:51 A.M.

"I want a list of every bottle collector in the state of Indiana," Agent Wallace ordered.

"Yes, sir. I'll get right on it." Lou Carson started toward the door but turned back. "Uh, Agent Wallace?"

"Yeah, Carson?"

"I was just thinking. If *wisdom* in the note was supposed to lead the kids to that broken bottle, didn't Sparrow have to plant it there?"

"Possibly, but where did Sparrow get the bottle?"

Carson nodded, "Good point, but he does live in a pre-Civil War mansion. It may have come with the territory."

"Possibly, but we need to check all leads."

"Yes, sir."

"And Carson."

"Yes, sir?"

"Search Sparrow's place again. Look for another bottle or receipt or anything connected to this Wise guy. And take the Fickle kids with you. My hunch about them was right."

"Yes, sir."

3:49 P.M.

Jacob raised the flowerpot on Professor Sparrow's back porch. "The key's missing!" he cried.

Deputy Carson tried the knob. The door swung open. He drew his pistol. "You kids wait here."

Jacob's fists clinched, alert and ready.

Isaac stood ready, too . . . ready to run . . . fast.

Elizabeth hopped and sidestepped to the imaginary rhythm of an Irish reel, oblivious to the possibility of impending danger.

Overhead, a vee of Canadian geese honked loudly. Isaac jumped. He watched the large birds sail toward Lake Monroe, Indiana's largest land-bound body of water. Professor Sparrow had promised to take the boys fishing there one day this fall. He wondered if "one day" would ever come now.

Deputy Carson reappeared. "Coast is clear. Nobody's in here. You guys can come in. Got any ideas where to look first?"

"The library?" Elizbeth suggested.

"No, the tunnel," Jacob said. "There's all kinds of Civil War stuff down there."

Carson shook his head. "No tunnel, today. That's the orders. Sorry, son."

"Kitchen?" Isaac said.

"Okay, Elizabeth," Deputy Carson said, "you and Jacob take the library. Isaac, you and I will search in here."

The library smelled of old leather. Dusty shelves packed with books hugged three walls. Elizabeth thumbed through *Story and Verse for Children* selected and edited by Miriam Blanton Huber, Ph.D. and published by The Macmillan Company in 1940.

"It feels like we're trespassing," she said. "Like we're invading Professor Sparrow's privacy."

Jacob opened another drawer in the oversized desk. "We're trying to save his life."

The scent of smoke from the old, stone fireplace hung heavy in the kitchen where Isaac rummaged through the pie safe. He noticed Professor Sparrow's empty rocker by the hearth. A wave of sadness washed over him.

Deputy Carson thumbed through papers on the table. "Hmm. Look at this." He held up *The Herald-Times*. September 27th was circled in red.

"Jacob's sixteenth birthday," Isaac said.

"Sparrow must have read Monday's paper before he vanished."

Isaac opened a cupboard stacked with Blue Willow china — white and blue plates, cups, and saucers embellished with plump, hand-painted birds over a Chinese pavilion and willow trees. "These were his mother's. Professor Sparrow said they came from an old inn in Maine."

Deputy Carson glanced up. "Nice."

The professor had told the boys his story. Benjamin Harrison Sparrow was born during the second World War in upstate New York to Theodore and Camellia Sparrow. At age eight, his family moved to Bar Harbor, Maine where his parents served as overseers at Hotel Bar Harbor.

The original structure on the waterside property was a clubhouse designed by William Ralph Emerson in 1887 (a cousin of Ralph Waldo Emerson) to promote literary and social culture. During World War II, the U.S. Navy had leased the building on Frenchman Bay as an observation headquarters. In 1947, the American Red Cross used it to shelter families who had lost homes in a city-wide fire. In 1950, the new hotel was built, which included a Reading Room and an additional 40-room wing. After his parents retired, the hotel was renamed Bar Harbor Inn.

Growing up in the quaint, New England town steeped in history had cultivated the professor's deep love for times gone by, which led to history degrees from Princeton and the University of Chicago as well as purchasing a civil-war mansion in Clear Creek, Indiana.

Isaac moved to the next cabinet.

"Glasses," he said.

Drawer by the sink.

"Forks and spoons and stuff."

He stirred through another drawer. "Hot pads and towels."

Under the sink.

"Sponges, Joy, Windex, Liquid Plumber, and what's this?"

Deputy Carson stopped examining the mail. "What's what?"

Isaac reached behind rusty pipes and pulled out a cobalt-blue J. Wise, Allentown, Pennsylvania soda bottle . . . with a note inside.

REFLECTIONS

POINT TO PONDER

Isaac found a message in a _____. If you had a

message for your family, where would you hide it?

PEARL FROM GOD

"You keep track of all my sorrows. You have collected all my

tears in Your bottle. You have recorded each one in Your

book." (Psalm 56:8 NLT)

PRINCIPLE TO LIVE BY

Psalm 56 refers to the time David was seized by the

Philistines in Gath. In grueling circumstances, David

trusted God and sang of His loving concern not only for

what was happening to David but also within him.

Beloved, the Lord takes note of every tear you shed. Go to

God in prayer and find grace to comfort and help you in

times of need.

Chapter 12:

Fishy, Fishy

Friday, 5:33 P.M.

"The note in the bottle said what?" Agent Wallace roared.

"Fishy, fishy in a brook. Daddy caught him with a hook," Lou Carson repeated.

Agent Wallace threw both hands in the air. "Yep, Sparrow's gone cuckoo for Cocoa Puffs."

"How do you know the old man wrote this one, too?" Carson asked.

"Look at the handwriting. Same as the first note."

On Mulberry Street, Isaac juggled a soccer ball in the backyard. "1091," he counted, "1092, 1093. You think Professor Sparrow's nuts?"

Jacob turned a flip on the trampoline. "Nope."

"How can you be so sure? Agent Wallace thinks he is."

1101.

1102.

1103.

"Think about it, Fish Fry."

"Why do you keep calling me that?"

"'Cause that's who you are — Fish Fry. That's who you've always been. Like I was saying, I know Professor Sparrow's not crazy 'cause we talked to him the Sunday before he disappeared, and he was just fine. You don't just go bonkers overnight. And besides, he wrote the notes weeks before that. The first one sounded a little crazy at first but made perfect sense once we figured it out."

"Yeah, you're right," Isaac said. "Whatcha think the second note means?"

1124.

1125.

"I don't know," Jacob said, "but we'll figure it out. Professor Sparrow left the clues for us, so they won't make sense to anybody else."

Isaac nodded. "I think that's why Agent Wallace asked us to help.

1134.

1135.

1136.

"What's your record, Fish Fry?"

"One thousand one hundred seventy-five."

1140.

1141.

1142.

"You might break your record today!"

1144.

1145.

1146.

"Fi-shy, fi-shy in-a-brook." Jacob jumped to the beat of the rhyme. "Brook . . . that could mean Clear Creek."

"Hey, yeah. But where would we start looking? It goes on for miles."

1154.

1155.

"1156," Isaac counted aloud. "I know! The creek runs near the history building where Professor Sparrow taught . . . uh, teaches. We could start there."

"Maybe."

1163.

1164.

1165.

Jacob bounced higher. "It also runs behind Professor Sparrow's house. I think we should start looking over there."

"Okay," Isaac agreed.

1168.

1169.

Jacob plopped down on the trampoline, his long legs hanging over the edge. "How can you talk and count at the same time?"

1171.

"Five more and you'll break your record!"

1173.

1174.

"Time for supper," Elizabeth yelled from the back deck.

Isaac glanced sideways. The ball hit the ground. "Aw, Elizabeth, look what you made me do!"

Jacob fell backwards laughing.

REFLECTIONS

POINT TO PONDER

Isaac is talented at _____ a soccer ball. What can you do well?

PEARL FROM GOD

"Then Moses summoned Bezalel and Oholiab and every skilled person to whom the LORD had given ability and who was willing to come and do the work." (Exodus 36:2)

PRINCIPLE TO LIVE BY

James 1:17 says that every good gift is from Father God. Exodus 36:2 teaches that although God gives people skills and abilities, people must be *willing* to work. What abilities has God given you, beloved? Are you willing to use your God-given abilities to help others and bring God glory?

Chapter 13:

Bang!

Saturday, 9:24 A.M.

Isaac cradled Summer like a baby. "You're so cute, kitty. I could just eat you up."

Meow.

Pretty Boy scurried from underneath the yew bush and curled around a bench leg where his boy sat.

Isaac set Summer on the ground beside him. "Here's your princess, Pretty Boy."

The cats kissed Eskimo style.

Mrs. Fickle opened the front door. "May I join you?"

Isaac moved over. "Sure."

A blue jay swooped toward the birdfeeder in the maple tree, scattering purple finches and a northern cardinal into the branches. Both cats crouched low in the grass, eyes glued on the feeder.

"Mom," Isaac groaned, "I feel as sad as a pickle in a pie."

She laughed. "How do you come up with such creative similes?"

He shrugged. "I don't know. They just pop out."

"So, why are you so sad, buddy?"

"Professor Sparrow's been missing three weeks now, and I'm afraid he's never coming back."

She nodded. "That makes me sad, too."

"You think he's still alive?"

Mrs. Fickle scooped Summer into her arms. "Well, the police are doing everything they can to find him, and

Professor Sparrow has an army of folks praying for him. So, I have hope."

Jacob rounded the corner. "You ready, Fish Fry?"

"Yep. Let me grab my bike," Isaac said.

Mrs. Fickle kissed his forehead. "Y'all be home by lunchtime and be careful."

"Thanks, Mom."

The boys dropped their bikes in the woods behind Professor Sparrow's fence. Jacob peered through the iron bars at the lonesome house. *I'll find you, Professor Sparrow. If it's the last thing I do on earth, I'll find you.*

They followed a deer trail to a line of moss-covered rocks and climbed down the bank to Clear Creek. Bright blades of sunlight sliced through the trees and into the water. Jacob picked up a flat stone and skipped it across the creek.

Isaac jumped to a rock midstream. Minnows darted underneath. "What are we looking for this time?"

Jacob shrugged. "Anything. Everything. The note said, 'Fishy, fishy in a brook.' Well, here's a brook. Then it said, 'Daddy caught him with a hook.' You see a fishing pole or line or bobber or something like that?"

Isaac hopped to the next rock. "Nope. What kind of fish are in this creek anyway?"

"Lots of bass — smallmouth, largemouth, spotted bass, rock bass. You name it. Why?"

"Just trying to figure out what in the world Professor Sparrow was trying to tell us."

"Hmm. Bass. Bass, bass in a brook. Daddy caught him with a hook." Jacob rolled his eyes. "Well, that didn't help." He threw another stone. Five skips spattered circles over the surface.

"Daddy caught him with a hook," Isaac repeated slowly. "Hey, I just thought of something. Remember our fishing trip last spring?"

"Yeah, when we caught all those bass and bluegills? And mom fried 'em that night with hush puppies and french fries. That was awesome!"

"Yeah!" Isaac said. "And Professor Sparrow and Mark had supper with us. Remember?"

Jacob skipped another rock. "So?"

"So, we didn't fish at Clear Creek that day," Isaac said. "We went to . . ."

A loud snap in the woods above made both boys wheel around. "Hey, who's up there?" Jacob called and scrambled up the creek bank.

Dirt and pebbles peppered Isaac's head as he grabbed for Jacob's ankle. "No, Jacob! Wait!"

Too late. Jacob vanished over the bank. Isaac heard crunching leaves under his brother's running feet.

"Wait!" Isaac hollered and clawed up the dirt wall.

At the top, he saw Jacob sprinting through the trees. Ahead of him, a man in a red-plaid jacket pushed through low-hanging branches and thorny vines.

"Stop!" Jacob yelled.

The man hesitated, then jerked something from a coat pocket.

BANG!!!

Isaac hit the ground and covered his head. Ears ringing. Heart pounding. When he looked up, his heart missed a beat. Twenty yards into the woods, Jacob sprawled on the ground — motionless.

"Jacob!" he screamed and crawled toward his brother.

REFLECTIONS

POINT TO PONDER

How do you think Isaac felt when he saw Jacob lying still on the ground? _____ Have you ever felt terrified? What did you do?

PEARL FROM GOD

"Do not be afraid of them; the LORD your God Himself will fight for you." (Deuteronomy 3:22)

PRINCIPLE TO LIVE BY

In the Bible, God tells you to look to Him and trust Him when you are afraid. He is always with you, beloved. He will help you. When you trust and obey God, He will use what you fear to teach you what you need.

Chapter 14:
AntikwT

10:14 A.M.

Lou Carson unwrapped a raspberry filled donut from Sugar Daddy's Cakes and Catering, his first chance for breakfast after three traffic stops and rescuing Bob's cat

from the roof of Stella's Place on Rogers Street. Just as he opened his mouth to take a bite, a dispatcher's voice crackled, "Unit 554."

Deputy Carson pressed the shoulder mic. "554, at intersection of West Church Lane and South Walnut Street. Go ahead."

Dispatcher: "554, respond to shots fired behind old Watt's mansion on Rabbit Road."

"10-4. En route." He hit the lights and siren. Deputy Carson knew Jacob and Isaac were there. He thought of his own kids and prayed, "Please, Lord, please let Jacob and Isaac be okay."

Protective instincts — the strong aspiration to keep others safe — was Lou Carson's driving force. On his eighteenth birthday his senior year of high school, he had registered for the U.S. Marine Corp and the day after graduation had left for boot camp on Parris Island off the coast of South Carolina. The training proved to be the most challenging thirteen weeks of his young life: intense swim qualifications, rifle qualifications, martial arts, physical fitness tests, combat training tests, academic tests for first-aid techniques as well as Marine Corp history, customs, and courtesies, and the infamous Crucible. The Crucible, the final grueling test before promoting from recruit to U.S. Marine, demanded a 54-hour, nine-mile hike carrying a heavy backpack and rifle with minimal food and limited sleep in the middle of Tropical Storm Gaston to boot.

From Parris Island, Private First-Class Lou Carson moved on to Combat School at Camp Geiger, North Carolina and deployed to Iraq soon after graduation. The following summer, he married Polly Fleming, his high school sweetheart. Upon his honorable discharge six years, four deployments, and many saved lives later, Gunnery

Sergeant Lou Carson was hired by the Monroe County Sheriff's Department and sent to the Indiana Law Enforcement Academy in Plainfield. Today, he and Polly were the proud parents of five — three boys and two girls — enough kids for their own basketball team.

Carson sped past Clear Creek Cemetery, lights flashing, siren blaring. Mrs. Fickle heard the wails. Color drained from her face. With trembling fingers, she punched Jacob's number into her phone.

"This is Jacob. Sorry I missed your call. Leave a message. Later gator."

She dropped to her knees.

"What's wrong, Mom?" Elizabeth asked.

"Sirens. I can't reach Jacob, and I have a bad feeling." Mrs. Fickle reached out a hand. "Pray with me?"

Elizabeth knelt beside her mother.

Tears blurred Isaac's eyes. "Jacob . . . Jacob, are you dead?"

Jacob rolled over. "No, Fish Fry, I'm not dead."

"Are you hurt? Did he shoot ya?"

Jacob jumped up and brushed leaves from his clothes. "Nope. Not shot. Not hurt."

Isaac punched his brother's arm. "You scared me to death! Why didn't you move when I called?"

Jacob nodded toward Professor Sparrow's house. "I just wanted that guy to think I was dead. Like in the Westerns. Come on. Let's go!"

The boys crept up the deer trail. A breeze rattled trees — the only sound in the forest silenced by the gunshot. At the edge of the woods, the sound of a motor roared from the driveway.

"Come on!" Jacob shouted.

They jumped the fence and raced to the front yard. A white chevy barreled down the drive toward Rabbit Road. Jacob whipped out his phone and snapped a picture.

Minutes later, Deputy Carson whipped into the driveway. On the front steps of Sparrow's house, Jacob and Isaac sat grinning like Cheshire cats.

Carson breathed a *thank You, Lord* and opened the door. "You guys okay? What happened?"

Jacob held up the phone. "Look what I got."

The picture showed a personalized license plate labeled "AntikwT" from the state of Maine. Deputy Carson enlarged the photo and tried to read it. "Anti . . . Antik. . . I don't get it."

"Antiquity!" Isaac blurted out. "You know, old relics and antiques and stuff. Like the blue soda bottles! I think we found our bottle collector. And something else. Professor Sparrow grew up in Maine."

146

Thunder rumbled in the distance.

"Storm's coming. Hop in, boys. I'll take you home and get your statements over there."

"What about our bikes?" Isaac asked.

"This way." Jacob motioned. "We can put 'em in the shed and pick 'em up later."

Deputy Carson trailed the boys around the house to a ramshackled tool shed. Inside, an earthy smell hung with the cobwebs. Professor Sparrow's frayed straw hat and dirty work gloves dangled on rusty nails by the door. Rakes, a hoe, two shovels, and a wheelbarrow lined the back wall. Under a cracked window, hammers, wrenches, and screwdrivers made a neat row across the workbench. A cabinet with cubby holes stood beside the bench. Dusty jars holding an assortment of nuts, bolts, nails, and screws sat in compartments that once held mail at the Clear Creek Post Office.

Jacob turned in circles. "Something's not right."

Deputy Carson glanced around. "Everything looks in order to me."

Jacob shook his head. "No, something's missin'."

"Professor Sparrow's missing," Isaac moaned. "We've never been in here without him."

"Something else." Jacob studied the floor.

The ceiling.

The walls.

"There." He pointed to an empty shelf behind the door. "His fishing gear's gone — tackle box, rods, reels, everything."

"Fishy, fishy in a brook," Deputy Carson muttered.

"Hey, guys, look at this." Isaac pulled a clear jar from a cubby hole and wiped the dust on his shirt. "It's got words like the blue bottles. It says, 'The Mason Jar of 1858 Trade Mark,' and there's a piece of paper inside."

Deputy Carson reached for the jar. "You've gotta be kidding me. Let me see that thing."

Carson unscrewed the lid and shook his head. "Another note."

"What's it say?" Jacob asked.

The deputy handed it to Jacob.

"'*The desire for gold is not for gold. It is for the means of freedom and benefit.*' Ralph Waldo Emerson."

REFLECTIONS

POINT TO PONDER

Deputy Carson's _____ force is protective instincts. What drives you? In other words, what motivates you most in life?

PEARL FROM GOD

"Not that I have already obtained all this, or have already arrived at my goal, but I press on to take hold of that for which Christ Jesus took hold of me . . . I press on toward the goal to win the prize for which God has called me heavenward in Christ Jesus." (Philippians 3:12,14)

PRINCIPLE TO LIVE BY

The driving force behind the Apostle Paul was the prize of eternal life with God through faith in His Son, Christ Jesus. Out of a heart of gratitude to God came a motivation to serve God and please Him in everything. Beloved, I pray that loving, serving, and pleasing God will be your driving force as well.

Chapter 15:
Gold Diggers

5:30 P.M.

Mrs. Fickle's head wagged. "No, no, a thousand times no. This whole special-agent deal has become *way* too dangerous."

"The guy didn't shoot *at* us," Jacob said. "I saw him with my own eyes. He just shot up in the air to scare us."

"I don't care. I don't want you boys anywhere near a stranger with a gun."

"But, Mom, we're so close to finding Professor Sparrow! We finally have a clue where he might be. Why can't we go with Deputy Carson tomorrow?" Jacob gave Mr. Fickle a pleading look. "Dad?"

Mr. Fickle took an apple slice from the red bowl on the kitchen table. "Let's enjoy dinner and talk about it later

— after we've all had time to calm down. Today was a bit unsettling for all of us."

Rain pattered against the kitchen windowpanes. Mr. Fickle placed the last dirty dish in the dishwasher while Mrs. Fickle wiped the countertops. "Ready?" he asked.

"Stephen, I really don't want the boys involved in this case anymore."

"I know, but we can't let fear determine our actions." He hugged her. "We have to seek God's will and trust Him."

She rested her head on his shoulder. "But it's just so dangerous. I'm scared, Stephen."

Mr. Fickle kissed her forehead. "I know, but let's pray about it as a family and take it one step at a time. Okay?"

Mrs. Fickle sighed. "Okay."

"Everybody to the living room!" Mr. Fickle called.

Jacob, Elizabeth, and Isaac didn't have to be called twice. The youngsters bounded up the stairs and plopped down on the couch. Lucy barked. Mr. Fickle patted the eleven-year-old Australian Shepherd. "Yes, you can come, too."

Mr. Fickle studied the faces of his children before speaking. *They're growing up so fast,* he thought. "Okay, so this decision we're facing isn't a matter of doing what you want or your mom wants or what I want. It's a matter of seeking God and doing what He wants. Agreed?"

"Yes, sir."

"Let's pray."

Heads bowed.

"Father, we love you so much," Mr. Fickle prayed. "Thank you for protecting Jacob and Isaac this morning. Please protect Professor Sparrow tonight and keep him safe. Guide us by to Your wisdom, Lord. Please show us what to do and help Deputy Carson and Agent Wallace find our friend. We love You so much, God. In Jesus' name we pray. Amen."

"Amen."

"Jacob, let's start with you. Tell us exactly what happened this morning."

"We were down at Clear Creek behind Professor Sparrow's house and heard a noise in the woods. So, I climbed up the bank and saw a guy crouching behind a tree. When I yelled, he ran, and I chased him. When I got close, he pulled out a gun and fired it up in the air."

"Yeah, I thought Jacob was dead," Isaac said.

Mrs. Fickle closed her eyes and drew a deep breath.

Mr. Fickle turned to Isaac. "What happened next, Isaac?"

"Well, I crawled over to Jacob to see if he was alive. Then we walked back to the house and saw a white pickup flying down the driveway."

"Hey," Elizabeth said, "didn't we see a white truck at Cedar Bluffs Nature Preserve? Remember, the one that looked like Grandpa's farm truck?"

"Yeah! I had a feeling somebody was watching us that day," Isaac said. "Anyway, back to this morning, Jacob got a picture of the license plate and called 911. While we were waitin' for Deputy Carson to get there, we figured out that A-N-T-I-K-W-T means antiquity."

"That's pretty smart," Mrs. Fickle said. "I'm impressed."

Isaac grinned. "Thanks, Mom. We think the guy's probably the bottle collector the police have been looking for. And he's from Maine where Professor Sparrow grew up, not Indiana. And that's not all! Professor Sparrow's

155

fishing stuff was missing from the tool shed. Wait, let me back up. The second note said, 'Fishy, fishy in a brook, Daddy caught him with a hook.' We thought the brook meant Clear Creek, but just before that guy showed up, I remembered our big fishing trip to Lake Monroe last spring. We think Professor Sparrow might be out at the lake somewhere."

Elizabeth wrinkled her nose. "You think Professor Sparrow's been fishing at Lake Monroe this whole time?"

Jacob rolled his eyes. "No, silly girl. We think Professor Sparrow left clues to tell us he was taken by force to Lake Monroe."

Elizabeth shook her head. "That doesn't make any sense. He had to write the notes before he left. So did he say something like, 'Uh, wait a minute, Mr. Kidnapper, I need to write some notes to Jacob and Isaac to let them know where you're taking me.'"

Mr. and Mrs. Fickle laughed.

"Well. . . no. I don't know," Jacob muttered.

"Remember? Mrs. Alice said he knew there might be trouble," Isaac said. "So, he must have written the notes just in case he was kidnapped."

"But how could he have known they would take him to Lake Monroe?" Elizabeth asked.

Her brothers shrugged.

"What about the note you found this morning?" Mrs. Fickle asked. "How did you find it, Isaac?"

"I was looking through the old cabinet from the Post Office and noticed that one of the jars looked different. Bigger and older. And it had raised letters like the blue bottles."

"What did today's note say again?" Mr. Fickle asked.

157

"*'The desire for gold is not for gold. It is for the means of freedom and benefit.'* It's quote by Ralph Waldo Emerson," Jacob explained.

"Have you guys figured out what that means?" Mr. Fickle asked.

"No, sir," Jacob said, "we were hoping you and Mom could help."

"Let's see." Mr. Fickle moved to the computer. "The blue bottle was made during the Civil War, and you said the jar you found in the shed was made in 1858. Right?"

"Yes, sir."

"So, both pieces came from around the same time period. And the note mentioned gold. Let's see what Google says about gold and the Civil War."

"That's a great idea, Dad!" Jacob said.

Mr. Fickle typed "Civil War gold."

"Bingo! According to Wikipedia . . . "

"Wikipedia?" Isaac groaned. "Seriously, Dad?"

Mr. Fickle grinned. "Just listen, bud. *'Confederate gold refers to hidden caches of gold lost after the American Civil War. Millions of dollars' worth of gold was lost or unaccounted for after the war, and its possible location has been the source of speculation of many historians and treasure hunters. When Union troops were on the verge of invading New Orleans, the Confederates quickly removed millions of dollars of gold to a safer location.'* And here's another site. It says that the gold was never found, and people continue to look for the lost treasure to this day."

"Maybe the guy's a treasure hunter," Isaac said, "and he hired those football players to dig in the tunnel 'cause he's looking for the Confederate gold. Does he think Professor Sparrow has it?"

"Possibly," Mr. Fickle said.

Jacob picked up his phone. "Can I call Deputy Carson?"

"*May* I call Deputy Carson," Mrs. Fickle corrected.

"May I?"

"No, buddy, it's getting late," Mrs. Fickle said. "You can talk to him at church tomorrow."

Jacob's face fell. "He won't be at church tomorrow. He'll be at Lake Monroe with the search team . . . where we ought to be, too."

"Please, Mom?" Isaac begged. "We're not the ones in danger. Professor Sparrow is, and Agent Wallace believes we can help find him."

Mrs. Fickle looked at her husband. "Stephen? What do you think?"

"Let's sleep on it and decide in the morning."

REFLECTIONS

POINT TO PONDER

Mr. Fickle said that God's _____ was more important than their wants. Have you ever had to choose between God's will and your wants?

PEARL FROM GOD

Jesus said, "I want Your will to be done, not mine." (Luke 22:42)

PRINCIPLE TO LIVE BY

In the Garden of Gethsemane, Jesus asked, "Father, if You are willing, please take this cup of suffering away from me. Yet I want Your will to be done, not mine." The next day, Jesus was beaten, nailed to a cross, and killed. His cup of suffering provided our chance for forgiveness and eternal life in heaven. No matter how much you want something, beloved, always pray for God's will to be done. Father God always knows best. Trust Him.

Chapter 16:
Danger for Christ's Sake

Sunday, 11:20 A.M.

After the offering plates were passed, Reverend Wheeler stepped to the pulpit. "Turn in your Bibles, please, to Second Corinthians chapter one verses eight through ten. Today, I'm reading from the New Living Translation. The Apostle Paul wrote: *We think you ought to know, dear brothers and sisters, about the trouble we went through. We expected to die . . .* "

Mrs. Fickle's mind wandered. *What if Jacob had . . . do not let yourself go there, Rebekah."*

"But as a result," Reverend Wheeler continued, *"we stopped relying on ourselves and learned to rely only on God . . ."*

Hey, that's the story Mrs. Alice told me, Isaac remembered.

Mrs. Fickle looked at her three children sitting beside her. *I want to rely on you, Lord. I really do, but when it comes to my kids, it's just so hard at times.*

"*He rescued us from danger,*" Reverend Wheeler read, "*and we have placed our confidence in Him.* May God bless the reading of His Holy Word. Let us pray."

Heads bowed.

"Heavenly Father," Reverend Wheeler prayed, "give us listening ears to hear and courageous hearts to obey. In Jesus' name we pray, Amen. Good morning, beloved."

"Good morning, pastor," the congregation replied in unison.

"I've entitled today's message: *Danger for Christ's Sake.*"

Mrs. Fickle's jaw dropped. Reverend Wheeler had her full attention.

"As most of you know," he said, "I grew up on a little farm just south of Clear Creek. My Pop was what you might call a bi-vocational farmer — full-time agriculturist and over-worked preacher."

Chuckles rippled.

"He pastored Smyrna Chapel down in Bedford for over forty years and was paid more in corn and potatoes than dollars or dimes. God called me to full-time ministry in 1963. I was fourteen years old. After Sunday evening service that winter night, Pop told Mama to take the other kids *and my coat* and drive on home, because he and I were walking. I felt as cold as a penguin on an iceberg."

Isaac snickered.

"Taking my coat away seemed ludicrous. I figured hard work and hard times had taken their toll. Pop had lost his ever-loving mind."

Mrs. Fickle frowned. *For goodness' sake. Why would any father make a child walk home in the cold without a coat?*

"I'd never seen Mama argue with Pop, but I sure hoped that night would be a first. It wasn't. She stuffed Sally, Joe, Milly, and my warm coat into our 1951 Ford pickup and drove off into the night, leaving Pop and me on the church steps. My teeth were chattering like an angry guinea pig."

Laughter.

"I'm not pulling your leg. Just look it up. Guinea pigs chatter their teeth when they're angry or agitated."

"I knew that," Elizabeth whispered in Isaac's ear.

"And, boy, was I ever agitated. I'd just committed my life to serving the Lord, and, as a reward, Pop was making me walk two miles in the freezing dark with no coat. If memory serves me right, it was eighteen degrees and snowing."

Mrs. Fickle shivered.

"We started down the frozen country road. Pop shed his own coat and wrapped it around my shoulders. He said, 'Son, a minister's life is not easy. God's work often brings criticism and hardships and can even mean walking hand in hand with danger.'"

Jacob and Isaac shot their mom a sideways glance. Mrs. Fickle's eyes were fixed on the pastor.

"I promise you, the second Pop said *danger*, a pack of wild coyotes commenced to yipping and howling and carrying on something fierce." Reverend Wheeler chuckled. "Every hair on my head stood up. I scooted closer to Pop. He put a strong arm around me and said, 'I wish I could shield you from the hardships ahead, son. I can't, but your heavenly Father will be right by your side. So, never be afraid to do whatever God tells you to do. He'll help you, and when your strength is gone, He'll give you His.' 'Like giving me your coat, Pop?' I asked. He smiled and assured me that God would supply my needs."

Mrs. Fickle nodded.

"Pop's pep talk that bitter cold February night fifty-eight years ago has proven true. Serving God is *not* easy whether you're a pastor, a mother, the butcher, the baker, or a candlestick maker, but the good Lord is faithful to His children. I can wholeheartedly testify today that God has never let me down, and the joy of serving Him has far outweighed all the troubles I've seen."

"Amen," Mrs. Fickle whispered.

Reverend Wheeler scanned the congregation. "Beloved, one of you may be facing a hard decision today."

Mrs. Fickle looked at Mr. Fickle. *Did Stephen tell Pastor Wheeler about the kids begging to go to Lake Monroe?*

"If you're at a crossroads, beloved, I encourage you to look for God's path and take it. If God is with you, then what is there to fear?"

Nothing, Mrs. Fickle answered silently.

"Don't hold back. Go forth with courage! Go forth for the sake of others. Go forth with God."

Applause rocked the rafters.

Mrs. Fickle whispered something in Mr. Fickle's ear. He smiled.

After the benediction, he leaned toward the kids. "Hurry to the van, guys. We're all going to Lake Monroe to find Professor Sparrow."

REFLECTIONS

POINT TO PONDER

Reverend Wheeler's Pop said that serving God may mean walking hand in hand with _____. Has doing the right thing ever put you in danger? What happened?

PEARL FROM GOD

"You light a lamp for me. The LORD, my God, lights up my darkness. In Your strength I can crush an army; with my God I can scale a wall." (Psalm 18:28-29 NLT)

PRINCIPLE TO LIVE BY

Beloved, ask Jesus to make you brave and courageous. Determine to do whatever the Lord tells you to do. Fear not. God is with you. Go forth with Him.

Chapter 17:

A Hunting We Will Go

12:33 P.M.

Five Fickles piled out of the minivan.

"Pack attack," Mr. Fickle ordered. "We stick together. We work together. Got it?"

"Yes, sir."

"I'll go pay for the canoes and meet you guys at the dock."

"I thought we were supposed to stick together," Isaac said.

"You know what I mean, Fish Fry." Mr. Fickle hurried off.

Jacob called after him, "What about Deputy Carson?"

"I texted him that we're going to the fishing hole . . . where daddy caught him with a hook." Mr. Fickle shook his head and muttered, "I can't believe I just said that."

At sunup, Agent Wallace divided a cohort of officers and K9 units into pairs for a door-to-door search for Amos Gilbert, the registered owner of a 2017 white, chevy pickup, Maine license plate: AntikwT.

"The suspect is a 51-year-old white male, six feet tall, medium build, mustache, brown hair, gray at the temples." He handed out maps. "We'll cover the marina, lodge, and all the cabins — private or rental — in the Lake Monroe vicinity. Your assigned area is circled in orange."

A stiff wind shook the trees, peppering leaves over the water. Elizabeth stepped into the canoe between Mr. and Mrs. Fickle. It tipped sideways.

"Whoa!" Mrs. Fickle said. "Careful, princess. It's too cold to go swimming today."

Jacob and Isaac were fifty yards out from the dock in a second canoe.

"Slow down, guys," Mr. Fickle called. "Stick together. Remember?"

Paddles pulled through choppy waves as the family pushed toward their favorite fishing spot. Lake Monroe was not a natural lake. The U.S. Army Corps of Engineers had dammed up Salt Creek in the early 1960s to create the 11,000-acre reservoir to prevent flooding downstream and serve as a primary water source for the city of Bloomington. It spread over two counties, Monroe and Brown. The Hoosier National Forest bordered much of the shoreline, and Ransburg Boy Scout Reserve sat on its eastern banks.

Mrs. Fickle pulled gloves from her jacket pocket. "Brrr-willy. I should have worn my winter coat. It's freezing!" She looked up. "Are those *snow* clouds?"

Elizabeth cocked her head toward the dark sky. "In October?"

Mrs. Fickle nodded. "It could happen. Remember Halloween night a few years ago when Grandpa and Grandma came up from Alabama? Rain turned to snow, and after five minutes of trick-or-treating, you guys begged to go home?"

"Yeah, Dad made hot chocolate with marshmallows. I wish I had some now."

At the fishing hole, Mr. Fickle pointed shoreward. "Pull up over there," he shouted over the wind. "We'll tie the canoes to a tree. We don't want to lose our rides back to the marina."

On land, Mrs. Fickle looked at Mr. Fickle. "So, what's the plan?"

Mr. Fickle looked at the kids. "Whatcha think, guys?"

"Start hunting," Jacob said and headed into the woods.

"Wait, Jacob," Isaac hollered, "think first. Why would Professor Sparrow bring us here?"

"You're wasting time, Fish Fry," Jacob grumbled.

"Look!" Elizabeth pointed through the trees. "Zoom Flume! I wish I had a can of spray paint."

The Zoom Flume was an abandoned waterpark built in the 1970s under a canopy of trees near Lake Monroe. It had closed in the 1980s. Rumor mill claimed the owner's high cost of liability insurance led to the shutdown.

Isaac pointed toward the flume. "Might as well start up there. It's the closest thing to the fishing hole."

A white flake landed on Elizabeth's blue jacket sleeve. "It's snowing!" she cried.

Mrs. Fickle studied the sky. "Oh, my."

A trail took the family to concrete steps and a walkway leading to the launch pad for the 480-foot flume now covered with scribbles and bright-colored doodles. Charred timbers from a structure that had burned to the ground strewn the forest floor. Midway down the graffitied chute, the flume narrowed to a forty-foot tunnel.

"Race you to the top!" Jacob yelled.

Jacob, Elizabeth, and Isaac scrambled up the chute. Mr. and Mrs. Fickle climbed the overgrown hill by way of steps and walkway.

At the pinnacle, the kids stopped dead in their tracks. A white male, medium build, brown hair, gray at the temples, mustache, and wearing a red-plaid, wool jacket sat on the concrete wall.

"About time you got here," Amos Gilbert growled.

REFLECTIONS

POINT TO PONDER

After the Zoom Flume closed in the 1980s, it was

_____. Have you ever felt abandoned? What's

your story?

PEARL FROM GOD

". . . *I have never seen the godly abandoned or their children*

begging for bread." (Psalm 37:25)

PRINCIPLE TO LIVE BY

Abandoned means deserted, rejected, neglected, and cast

off. In the book of Hebrews, God promised, "I will never

fail you. I will never abandon you." So, beloved, you can

say with confidence, "The Lord is my helper, so I will not

be afraid."

Chapter 18:

Cold Giblet Gravy

12:38 P.M.

Mrs. Alice added sunflower seeds to the birdfeeder and shuffled back inside. "Silly old woman," she muttered, "rambling around this place all by yourself when you could be at Lake Monroe helping Isaac."

Meow.

"What do you think, Morton. Shall I go?"

Meow.

"I agree." She hurried to the hall closet and shook mothballs from a wool, winter coat. Bundled, booted, gloved, and scarved, Mrs. Alice grabbed her pocketbook and started for the carport.

"Wait. Glasses. Where are my glasses?"

Meow.

Mrs. Alice fumbled through her purse. Checked the nightstand by her bed. The kitchen table. Rocking chair. Rummaged through her purse again. "Where in the world did I put 'em, Morton?" She asked and laid a hand on top of her head. There sat her glasses under the green scarf. "I sure do miss my mind," she muttered.

Gertie spit and sputtered down State Road 446, hitting every pothole in the pavement. The dinked and dented jalopy had been quite the beauty back in the day — four-door luxury sedan with a black vinyl top, sleek copper-colored limousine body, lace-spoke hub caps, automatic V8 engine, and a shiny chrome front hood ornament — a thirtieth wedding anniversary gift from J. W.

Mrs. Alice patted the cracked dashboard. "You can do it, old girl. Almost there."

She leaned forward, squinting. "Zoom Flume trail is just ahead. I'll hike from there."

Gertie backfired.

"Don't you worry about me, Gertie girl. I know this place like the back of my hand. We brought the kids here bajillions of times before you even hit the assembly line."

Mrs. Alice whipped off the road and mashed the brakes. Gertie's front bumper banged into a white pickup truck.

"Oops, sorry," she spluttered. "Cane or no cane? What do you think, Gertie?" Peeping through the foggy windshield at the budding winter wonderland, Mrs. Alice grabbed the walking stick and opened the door.

A well-worn path climbed a hill and disappeared into the woods. "*'Continuous, unflagging effort, persistence and determination will win.'* James Whitcomb Riley," she quoted and then hit the trail with determination.

Mrs. Alice paused midway up the rise.

Huffing.

Puffing.

Huffing.

Puffing.

The path fell over a gentle knoll and then rose steeply. "'*After climbing (huff puff) a great hill, one only finds that there are many more (huff puff) hills to climb*.' Nelson (huff puff) Mandela," she panted. "You can do it, old girl. You can do '*all things (huff puff) through Christ (huff puff) who strengthens you*.' Apostle Paul, Philippians four (huff puff) thirteen. Here we go!"

1:13 P.M.

Jacob stomped toward the stranger. "Hey, you're the guy I chased through the woods."

"Maybe."

Jacob pointed a finger in his face. "You shot at me!"

"Misfire."

Elizabeth hollered, "Dad!!!"

"Right behind you, Lizzie Lou." Mr. Fickle stepped in front of her and stretched a hand toward the stranger. "Stephen Fickle."

The man ignored the gesture.

"Where's Professor Sparrow?" Jacob demanded.

"You tell me," Amos Gilbert snarled.

Mrs. Fickle eased her phone from a pocket and clicked.

Gilbert stood up. "I wouldn't do that if I were you, ma'am."

Mr. Fickle stepped closer. "Is that a threat, sir?"

Isaac was shaking like a wet dog and kicking himself for suggesting they search the Zoom Flume. Quicker than a cheetah, scrawny fingers suddenly appeared out of nowhere, clutched his jacket, and jerked the boy into Indiana hemlock branches.

1:16 P.M.

Deputy's Carson's phone buzzed. Rebekah Fickle's name appeared on the screen. A loud crash answered his hello.

"Rebekah? Rebekah, you there?"

Dead silence.

The deputy hit the recall button.

"This is Rebekah. Leave a message and have a great day with Jesus."

Carson punched in Jacob's number.

"This is Jacob. Sorry I missed your call. Leave a message. Later gator."

Stephen's cell phone.

"You have reached Stephen Fickle. Please leave your name and number, and I will return your call at my earliest convenience."

Carson hit the shoulder mic. "Unit 554 to Agent Wallace."

Crackle. "Agent Wallace. Go ahead."

"Requesting watercraft to search Lake Monroe. Fickle family in possible trouble. I repeat, Fickle family in trouble."

"Ten four. Meet at Lake Monroe Marina 1400 hours."

Seventeen minutes later, Deputy Carson found Agent Wallace in a twenty-foot Starcraft ski boat with an outboard, 200-horsepower, Mercury motor.

"Hop in, Carson," Wallace ordered. "Destination?"

"West toward the old Zoom Flume."

"Zoom what?"

"Zoom Flume, an abandoned waterpark. It's near the Fickle's fishing spot."

They powered through the no-wave zone. Carson pointed ahead. "Watch out for those logs."

At closer range, "logs" transformed into two canoes bobbing on the waves. Wallace pulled back the throttle. Carson leaned over the side of the boat and caught the rope tied to the end of one canoe. He held up the loose end. "It's been cut. Looks like the Fickles have been sabotaged.

The missing-professor saga thickened like cold giblet gravy.

REFLECTIONS

POINT TO PONDER

How would you describe Mrs. Alice? What have you done

that required determination and grit?

PEARL FROM GOD

". . . the gracious hand of his God was on him because Ezra

determined in his heart to study and obey the Law of the

LORD and to teach those decrees and regulations to the

people of Israel." (Ezra 7:9-10)

PRINCIPLE TO LIVE BY

Determination is the strong will or resolve to persevere

toward a difficult goal despite challenging obstacles. An

Old Testament prophet named Ezra determined in his

heart to study, obey, and teach the Law of the LORD.

Beloved, today, will you determine in your heart to know,

obey, and share God's Word with others?

Chapter 19:

Jack's Cave

1:37 P.M.

Jaw-locking fear froze the squeal in Isaac's throat. The boy crashed through hemlock needles and landed by yellow galoshes beneath a wool, winter coat that smelled of mothballs. He looked up at a wild-eyed Mrs. Alice with a crooked finger pressed to her lips. She motioned for him to follow. They crept from boulder to boulder, pausing for Mrs. Alice to catch her breath behind each tall rock.

Two hundred yards west of the flume, Isaac whispered, "Where we going?"

"Jack's . . . Cave," she wheezed and pointed ahead to a yawning hole in the rocky bluff.

Locals claimed that Jack's Cave was a historic landmark, once serving as a hideout for Hoosier Union soldiers during the War Between the States. In 1863, Brigadier General John Hunt Morgan marched Confederate cavalrymen from Tennessee, across Kentucky, and into southern Indiana. Morgan sent detachments north to make the Union believe Southern troops were headed for Indianapolis. In defense, the Union planted infantry along the projected route. One unit allegedly hid in the cave for over a month, living off fish from Lake Monroe.

Morgan's raid, however, ran a different course — from Corydon, Indiana to Mt. Vernon and then on into Ohio — 1,000 miles from start to finish. The Hoosier Blues in Jack's Cave never laid eyes on a Johnny Reb (the Union's nickname for soldiers of the Confederacy).

Inside the cave, it appeared someone had been hiding there today. Embers smoldered in a dying campfire. A sleeping bag sprawled across the packed-clay floor. Cans, empty water bottles, and dirty clothes were thrown here, there, and yonder.

Isaac heard gurgles from an underground stream deeper within the cave. He jumped when a droplet from the ceiling hit his forehead. "We gotta get Deputy Carson. Do you have a cell phone, Mrs. Alice?"

"I think so." She opened her pocketbook. "Should be one in here somewhere. The kids made me get it, but I never did learn how to use the confounded thing." She pulled out an eyeglass case. "Nope, that's not it. Wait a minute." She dug deeper. "Here! Here it is."

Isaac grabbed the phone and flipped it open. "Battery's dead," he groaned. "I didn't know anybody still had flip phones. When was the last time you charged it?"

"Was I supposed to charge it?" she asked.

"Never mind. How did you get here, Mrs. Alice?"

"Gertie."

"Where's Gertie now?"

"Parked down the hill on the side of the road."

"Then why did we come to Jack's Cave?"

She shrugged. "It seemed like a good idea at the time."

Isaac tugged Mrs. Alice's arm. "Come on. Let's go."

She planted her cane firmly in the clay. "No, wait. We can't risk that ghastly Amos Gilbert seeing us."

"How do you know his name?"

"Never mind that for now, Isaac. Other way," Mrs. Alice said, pointing behind them.

Isaac stared into the black hole. "What do you mean other way?"

"Jack's Cave is a tunnel. It runs about a half mile straight through the ridge. There's another entrance on the other side about a mile from the Marina."

A flashback of Brough's Tunnel at Clifty Falls made him go weak in the knees. "No!! . . . no, ma'am! That's impossible! It's pitch black in there! We can't do it!"

"You're half right. I can't do it, but *you* can. It'd take me till Christmas to get to through the caverns on this cane, but you're young and strong and fast, Isaac. You have to go for help."

"No!!! It's too hard. I can't see! I can't do it!"

"Isaac, look at me. Yes, you can. What did Nelson Mandela say? *'The brave man is not he who does not feel afraid, but he who conquers that fear.'* Remember, Isaac, God is with you."

His voice raised an octave. "I don't even have a light!"

Mrs. Alice pulled a little Eveready flashlight from the side pocket of her purse.

"But what if the batteries . . . "

"New batteries. They won't die and neither will you."

"But . . ."

"No buts, Isaac. You can do this. You *have* to do this. Your family needs your help and so do I. Be brave and remember, child, God is with you. Now go!" She gave him a gentle shove. "When you come out the back entrance, just follow the trail. It'll take you straight to the Marina."

Isaac took the flashlight. His hand shook so hard he almost dropped it as he disappeared into the darkness.

"Help him, Lord Jesus," Mrs. Alice whispered.

REFLECTIONS

POINT TO PONDER

In the story, Jack's Cave is a historic _____. Have

you visited a historic landmark? What memorable event

took place there? What's your best memory of that visit?

PEARL FROM GOD

*"I remember the days of old. I ponder all Your great works. I
think about what You have done." (Psalm 143:5 NLT)*

PRINCIPLE TO LIVE BY

A landmark is a place or object marking a past important
event. In Joshua chapter 4, the LORD commanded His
children to take up twelve stones from the Jordan River,
one stone for each of the twelve tribes. Years later when
their children asked, "What do these stones mean?" God's
people said, "These stones mark the day the Lord cut off
the flow of the Jordan River and His people crossed over to
the Promised Land." Beloved, why not start a landmark
journal and record the wonderful deeds God does for you?
Who knows? Maybe your kids will read it one day and
praise the Lord.

Chapter 20:

Brave

The passageway narrowed like a keyhole between jagged rocks. Isaac turned sideways. A sharp point snagged his jacket. He jerked loose and scooted on through. Past the squeeze, the walls spread to an open grotto.

"Don't think. Just keep going," he told himself and checked his watch — 2:04 P.M.

The boy's echoing footsteps conjured images of plaid-jacket man creeping up behind him. He quickened his pace and tripped facedown, slamming a knee into a sharp rock. The flashlight flew from his hand and clanked against limestone. The sound bounced from stalagmite to stalactite and faded into the caverns.

Isaac crawled toward the shiny beacon, snatched up the flashlight, and peeked at his jeans. Blood spotted the pants leg. "I'm not brave," he whimpered and then shouted, "I'm not brave!"

"BRAVE."

"BRAve."

"Brave," Jack's Cave answered.

Isaac pressed on, following the thin beam down the meandering pathway. Babbles of the underground stream escalated to a roar. The light found a rushing river.

"'*The river's story flowing by, forever sweet to ear and eye, forever tenderly begun — forever new and never done.*' James Whitcomb Riley." Isaac slapped himself upside the head. "Oh, man. I'm turning into Mrs. Alice."

The path disappeared into the water and reappeared on the other side. *Too far to jump. Too cold to swim. How am I ever gonna get across that thing?* he wondered.

Isaac scanned the rock walls from floor to high ceiling. To the right. To the left. Ten yards left, he discovered a stone formation high above his head — a natural bridge over the water.

Fissures scarred the support wall, creating a hand-and-foothold ladder. He looped the flashlight's leather strap around his wrist and took a deep breath. "You can do this. You have to do this, Fish Fry."

Isaac jammed a tennis shoe into a crack, reached for a crevice overhead, and pushed up. His foot slipped, crashing him to the cave floor.

"I can't do this!" he cried.

"THIS."

"THis."

"This."

"Help me, Lord Jesus!"

"JESUS."

"JESus."

"Jesus."

Mrs. Alice's voice rang in his mind. "Your family needs your help and so do I."

"It's too hard!" Isaac yelled.

"HARD."

"HArd."

"Hard," Jack's Cave mocked.

Isaac buried his face in his hands. Sobs racked his shoulders and ricocheted through the chambers. He cried till his eyes ran dry. Wiping his nose on the back of his hand, he snubbed, "Okay, God is with me. God is with me. Remember, God is always with me." He threw his head back. "God, please be with me!"

The cave echoed, "ME!"

"Me."

"Me."

He drew a ragged breath. "God is with me." Isaac dug a finger into the clay and, like a linebacker for the Indianapolis Colts, drew a line of mud under each eye. "You have to do this, Fish Fry. Now, trust God and . . . and . . . sing!"

The boy warbled the only old hymn he knew by heart — Mrs. Alice's favorite: "Victory in Jesus."

"I heard an old, old story,
How a Savior came from glory."

Standing.

"How He gave His life on Calvary
To save a wretch like me."

Foot on the stone wall.

"I heard about His groaning,
Of His precious blood atoning."

Pushing up.

"Then I repented of my sins
And won the victory."

Climbing.

"O victory in Jesus.
My Savior forever."

Climbing.

"He sought me and bo't me
With His redeeming blood."

Higher.

"He loved me ere I knew Him
And all my love is due Him."

On the bridge.

"He plunged me . . . "

Crawling.

"To victory . . . "

Crawling.

"Beneath the cleansing flood."[2]

"Don't look down."
Standing.
"Don't look down."
Running!!

---

[2] VICTORY IN JESUS, E. M. Bartlett, 1939.

REFLECTIONS

POINT TO PONDER

What stretched across the underground river in Jack's Cave? A natural _____.

Do you believe that Jesus is the only bridge to God and heaven? Why or Why not?

PEARL FROM GOD

"Jesus told him, 'I am the way, the truth, and the life. No one can come to the Father except through Me." (John 14:6)

PRINCIPLE TO LIVE BY

The *only* way to God and His Kingdom is Jesus Christ. The Bible says: *"For everyone has sinned; we all fall short of God's glorious standard." (Romans 3:23). "And the wages of sin is death, but the free gift of God is eternal life through Christ Jesus our Lord" (Romans 6:23). "Everyone who calls on the name of the LORD will be saved!" (Romans 10:13).* Beloved, have you called on the Lord Jesus and received His free gift of life, forgiveness, and eternity with Him?

Chapter 21:

Like the Wind

2:45 P.M.

On the far side of the river, Isaac found a lofty chamber festooned in rock art. Water cascaded flowstone shaped like a pumpkin. A mighty stalagmite rose before him like a giant haystack. Straw-like stalactites less than one centimeter in diameter hung from the ceiling. Thin, translucent calcite deposits resembling strips of crispy bacon clung to the high dome.

Isaac switched off the Eveready. Blackness surrounded him like an inky blanket. He couldn't see his hand in front of his face, which meant he was still in the dark zone where no daylight reached.

How much farther? he wondered.

The boy followed a zig-zagged path around floor-to-ceiling columns, dripholes, swirlholes, and pools. Just when he was beginning to feel like an expert spelunker, his new-found courage fizzled. The chamber split in two.

What if I pick the right shaft, and it's the wrong way?

Or the left shaft, and it's the wrong way?

What if I get lost?

What if I never get out of this stupid cave?

And die of starvation?

And nobody ever finds me?

Or my family?

Or Mrs. Alice?

Or Professor Sparrow?

What if . . .

What if . . .

He stopped himself.

What if I just calm down and ask God for help?

Isaac shut his eyes, switched off the flashlight, and prayed. When he opened them again, a dim glow filled the right shaft — the twilight zone, the part of a cave that receives a smidgen of sunlight because it's near an entrance.

He jumped up and down. "Thank You, thank You, thank You, Lord Jesus!!!"

"JESUS!!"

"JESus!"

"Jesus," Jack's Cave praised.

Outside, the snow had stopped falling. A trail from the cave's back door skirted a large, round rock powdered white. *Looks like a donut*, Isaac thought. His stomach growled.

He checked the time — 3:57 P.M. Three hours to sundown and only a mile to the Marina. *Easy peasy*, he thought.

Last year, Isaac had set the mile-run record for fifth graders at his school: six minutes and forty-six seconds on a flat, paved track. Running up and down icy hills would take twice as long — at least.

The boy raced like his family's lives depended on it. Maybe they did. Sprinting down the hill, he fell three times. His knee ached. His heart pounded. His breath came in short, raspy gasps, but he ran like the wind.

A rocky creek through the ravine at the bottom of the hill divided the trail. Isaac hopped from stone to stone and sped up the next rise. At the top, the footpath dropped drastically toward Lake Monroe.

He slowed.

Eyes fixed on the snow-powdered path.

Concentrating.

Carefully, he worked his way down the slippery descent. The woods thinned where the trail flattened and rounded the lakeshore. In the distance, Isaac saw docks sticking out in the water with boats tethered to the sides. The sound of a motor drew his eyes to the middle of the lake. A boat towing two canoes sped toward the Marina.

"Deputy Carson!" Isaac jumped up and down and waved his arms. "Over here!!" he yelled.

The noise drowned his cries. The boat sped on.

Isaac ran parallel to the fastmoving vessel.

Screaming.

Waving.

Praying.

REFLECTIONS

POINT TO PONDER

What did Isaac do to be heard? Do you sometimes feel like God doesn't hear your prayers? What do you do to be heard?

PEARL FROM GOD

"In those days when you pray, I will listen. If you look for Me wholeheartedly, you will find Me." (Jeremiah 29:12-13)

PRINCIPLE TO LIVE BY

God listens to the prayers of the wholehearted. However, Psalm 66:18 says, *"If I had not confessed the sin in my heart, the Lord would not have listened."* The word "sin" means missing the mark — doing something God said not to do or not doing something He said to do. The word "confess" means to agree with God that my actions are wrong. First John 1:9 tells us that *"if we confess our sins to [God], He is faithful and just to forgive us our sins and to cleanse us from all wickedness."* Beloved, confess your sins and pray to Him with a whole heart. He's listening!

Chapter 22:
Team Isaac

4:19 P.M.

Deputy Carson tapped Agent Wallace's shoulder. "Stop!"

Agent Wallace pulled back the throttle.

"Did you hear something?"

On shore, Isaac bounced up and down, waving both arms and screaming at the top of his lungs, "Over here!!! Over here!!!"

"Isaac??" Deputy Carson cupped his hands around his mouth. "We're coming, Isaac! Hang on, buddy."

Wallace gunned the motor, leaving the canoes behind, rocking in the wake.

"Slow down. It gets shallow here," Carson yelled.

Wallace cut the engine. The boat rocked back and forth.

"You okay, Isaac?" Carson hollered.

"Yes, sir. Uh, no, sir. A mean man has my family!"

Carson looked both ways and pointed to a dock. "Meet us over there. We'll pick you up."

In the boat, Agent Wallace held up a photo of Amos Gilbert and fired questions at the boy like a machine gun. "Is this the man?"

"Yes, sir."

"Where's he holding your family?"

"Zoom Flume," Isaac answered.

"Did he have a gun."

"No, sir, I didn't see a gun."

Wallace spotted the blood on Isaac's jeans. "What happened?"

"I tripped in the cave."

"Cave? What cave?" Wallace asked.

"Jack's Cave where Mrs. Alice is."

"Alice Holtzhausen is in Jack's Cave??" Deputy Carson asked incredulously.

"Yes, sir."

Wallace turned to the deputy. "Carson, how do you get to the Zoom Flume by land?"

"State Road 446. Park at the State Recreation Area, cross the highway, and climb the hill."

Isaac nodded. "Yes, sir. That's where Mrs. Alice left Gertie."

"Gertie??" roared Agent Wallace. "Who in the Sam Hill is Gertie?"

"Mrs. Alice's old car."

Wallace frowned and pressed his shoulder mic. "Agent Wallace to all units. Suspect has been spotted near the old Zoom Flume. All units report to the SRA on State Road 446 and wait for orders. I repeat. All units report to State Recreation Area on 446. Suspect is possibly armed and possibly holding Fickle family against their will."

In minutes, Team Isaac grew from a sixth grader and a granny to a swarm of trained law enforcement officers.

4:33 P.M.

Mrs. Alice heard the sirens from Gertie's driver's seat and breathed a sigh of relief. "He made it!" She whispered heavenward, "Thank You, Lord."

Amos Gilbert heard sirens, too — from inside Jack's Cave. When he realized the smallest Fickle had flown the coup, he had panicked, confiscated the family's cell phones, and fled to the cave like a man with his hair on fire, leaving four bewildered Fickles behind at the Zoom Flume.

Isaac's family heard the siren wails from deep in the woods where they were frantically searching and praying for Isaac.

Mr. Fickle pointed west. "They're coming from that way. Let's go!"

Deputy Carson's patrol car screeched to a halt beside Gertie. Isaac hopped from the backseat just as his family burst from the trees.

"Mom!"

Four Fickles were on the boy like chickens on a June bug — hugging and kissing and crying all at the same time.

"Where have you been?" Mrs. Fickle asked.

Jacob put Isaac in a headlock and ruffled his hair. "Good to see you, Fish Fry. How did you find Deputy Carson?"

Agent Wallace interrupted the reunion. "Where's Gilbert?"

Mrs. Alice rolled down the window. "Probably hiding in Jack's Cave."

"Where's Jack's Cave?" Wallace demanded.

Isaac stepped forward. "I'll show you, sir."

Mr. Fickle and Jacob joined Isaac. Agent Wallace held up a hand. "Only the boy," he said. "Too many civilians will only get in the way."

4:54 P.M.

"There," Isaac whispered, pointing to the yawning hole in the rocky bluff.

Agent Wallace motioned his men forward then pushed Isaac behind a rock. "Stay here," he ordered. "And don't move."

Officers flanked both sides of Jack's Cave.

"Amos Gilbert," Agent Wallace shouted through a bullhorn. "You're surrounded. Come out peacefully with your hands over your head."

Silence.

"Don't make it harder on yourself, Gilbert. Come on out and talk to us. It'll be better for you if you cooperate."

A tug on the agent's sleeve made him whirl around. "Isaac! I told you to stay put! Now, get out of here!" Wallace roared.

"But . . . but Mr. Gilbert's not surrounded, sir. There's another opening to the cave on the other side of the ridge."

"You sure?"

"Yes, sir, that's how I got out. And an underground river runs through the middle. I climbed the wall and crawled across a stone bridge."

"Hmm," Wallace said thoughtfully. "Can you find the back entrance again?"

"Yes, sir. It's behind the donut rock."

"Deputy Carson!" Wallace yelled.

Carson hurried over. "Yes, sir?"

"Take another officer and a K-9 unit and go with Isaac to the back entrance of the cave."

Carson looked at the boy and nodded. "Yes, sir."

"If we can't talk Gilbert out the front, we'll flush him out the back."

"How?" Isaac asked.

"Tear gas. Carson, you and your men be ready."

Agent Wallace put a hand on Isaac's shoulder. "And tie

this one to a tree if you have to but make sure he's safe and out of the way."

"Yes, sir," Carson said. "Let's go, Isaac."

5:29 P.M.

"Agent Wallace to Deputy Carson."

Carson hit the shoulder mic. "Carson here. Go ahead, sir."

"Suspect coming your way," Agent Wallace said. "I repeat, suspect moving toward back cave exit."

"Roger. We're ready, sir."

Isaac peeked around the donut rock.

Deputy Carson motioned him out of sight.

5:52 P.M.

The K-9 growled. Seconds later, a coughing, wheezing, snorting, soaked-to-the-bone Amos Gilbert stumbled out of Jack's Cave. Deputy Carson leaped from his hiding place, tackled him to the ground, and pulled the man's arms behind his back. The K-9 officer slapped handcuffs on the suspect's wrists.

"You have the right . . . to remain silent," Deputy Carson said between deep breaths. "Anything you say can . . . and will . . . be used against you in a court of law. You have the right to an attorney . . . If you cannot afford an attorney, one . . . will be provided for you. Do you understand the rights I have just read to you?"

Gilbert nodded.

"Speak up," Carson shouted.

"Yeah (cough), I understand."

6:30 P.M.

"Mr. Fickle, I'll need you to come down to the station and give your statement," Agent Wallace said.

Mr. Fickle shook the agent's hand. "Happy to. Thank you, Agent Wallace. Good job."

Patrol cars rolled down snow-covered State Road 446 like a Christmas parade. Mrs. Alice called out the window, "Well, looks like the party's over. Climb in before you all freeze to death. Gertie and I will take you back to Isaac and your van."

"Thanks, Mrs. Alice," Mr. Fickle said. "Would you like me to drive?"

Jacob glared at the white pickup truck sitting nose to nose with Gertie. "But where's Professor Sparrow? That's what I wanna know!"

REFLECTIONS

POINT TO PONDER

When Agent Wallace asked for directions to Jack's Cave,

who volunteered to show him the way? _____

Has Isaac changed in the story? What helped him change?

What needs to change in your life?

PEARL FROM GOD

"And so, dear brothers and sisters . . . give your bodies to God because of all He has done for you . . . Don't copy the behavior and customs of the world, but let God transform you into a new person by changing the way you think. Then you will learn to know God's will for you, which is good and pleasing and perfect." (Romans 12:1-2 NLT)

PRINCIPLE TO LIVE BY

Want to change your life, beloved? Seek God, trust God, and do what He says. *"May God Himself, the God of peace, sanctify you through and through. May your whole spirit, soul, and body be kept blameless at the coming of our Lord Jesus Christ. The One who calls you is faithful, and He will do it!" (1 Thessalonians 5:23-24)*

Chapter 23:
The Mostest Fun

6:57 P.M.

As the sun slipped under the horizon, Gertie slipped as smooth as Indiana molasses into a parking space at the Lake Monroe Marina. Mr. Fickle put her in park and switched off the key.

Isaac ran over to meet them. A big grin covered his face. "We got him!" he hollered.

"Good job, Isaac!" Mrs. Alice said. "I knew you could do it! I'm so proud of you."

"Mrs. Alice, how did you get out of the cave and back down the hill?" the boy asked.

"A while after you left, I decided the cave might not be the safest place if Mr. Gilbert came back. So, I snuck out and slipped and slid my way back to Gertie.

Now, I have something for you," Mrs. Alice said, digging in her pocketbook. "Where did I put that thing?" She dumped the contents into her lap and picked up an envelope. "Here."

"What's that?" Isaac asked.

Her green eyes sparkled. "The last clue."

"Ma'am???"

"The last clue to finding Professor Sparrow."

Isaac took the envelope. Jacob jerked it from his hand. "Let me see that, Fish Fry."

"Jacob," Mrs. Fickle said, "call your brother Isaac."

Isaac grinned. "It's okay, Mom. I decided I like my nickname."

"When did you decide that?" Mrs. Fickle asked.

"Back in the cave."

Jacob's eyebrow raised. "How come?"

"Well, when I was all alone in the dark, I realized that the people who gave me that nickname love me. And I love them."

"I *love* you, Fish Fry!" Elizabeth said dramatically, then yanked the note from Jacob. "Here. Let me read it."

"Little Orphant Annie's come to our house to stay,

An wash the cups and saucers up,

an brush the crumbs away,

An' shoo the chickens off the porch,

an' dust the hearth, an' sweep,

An' make the fire, an' bake the bread,

an earn her board-an'-keep;

An' all us other childern, when the supper things is done,

We set around the kitchen fire an' has the mostest fun." [3]

---

[3] JAMES WHITCOMB RILEY, "Little Orphant Annie," 1885.

"James Whitcomb Riley," Mrs. Fickle and Mrs. Alice blurted at the same time.

Isaac gasped. "I know where Professor Sparrow is!"

REFLECTIONS

POINT TO PONDER

Mrs. Alice gave Isaac the last _____ to finding Professor Sparrow. If you were writing this story, where would Isaac find the lost professor?

PEARL FROM GOD

"And when [the shepherd] has found [his lost sheep], he will joyfully carry it home on his shoulders. When he arrives, he will call together his friends and neighbors, saying, 'Rejoice with me because I have found my lost sheep. In the same way, there is more joy in heaven over one lost sinner who repents and returns to God than over ninety-nine others who are righteous and haven't strayed away." (Luke 15:5-7 NLT)

PRINCIPLE TO LIVE BY

Luke 19:10 says that Jesus Christ came to seek and to save the lost. In other words, Jesus came to earth to find people separated from God by sin (the lost) and rescue (save) them. Do you need rescuing, beloved? Trust what Jesus did for you. Ask Him to save you and believe that He will do it!

Chapter 24:

Rat Trap

Five Weeks Earlier

Saturday, 11:11 A.M.

Mrs. Alice jammed her fists into skinny hips. "That's ludicrous, Ben Sparrow! You'll be tarred and feathered and run out of town on a rail."

Professor Sparrow chuckled. "Just trust me and when trouble hits the fan, give the first note to the boys. Better yet, give it to the one smart enough to ask for help."

"How do you know one of them will ask me for help?"

"They will. You helped them find the tunnels, didn't you?"

"And just what are you hoping to accomplish, you crazy old coot?"

Professor Sparrow made his eyebrows dance. "To catch a crooked rat in his own trap."

Mrs. Alice laid a hand on his shoulder. "Please, Ben, just give the man what he wants."

The professor spread his hands with a shrug. "I don't have what he wants, Alice, and I've told him that a hundred times. Here. Take these." He put four envelopes in Mrs. Alice's hand and kissed it.

Worry crinkled her face more. "Where will you be?"

"That's for me to know and you and the boys to figure out," he said and walked out the door.

A white pickup with an "AntikwT" license plate was sitting by the gates when the professor got home. Professor Sparrow rolled down the window of the old Galaxy 500. Amos Gilbert hopped from the truck.

"Well, Mr. Gilbert," Professor Sparrow said, "you've finally convinced me. I'm ready to cooperate."

Gilbert sneered. "Finally came to your senses, huh?"

Sparrow held out an envelope. "I've seen the light!"

"This it?"

"Yes, a map to the gold. Now, will you leave me alone?"

The man snatched the parcel and climbed in his truck. "This better be legit, old man, or you haven't seen the last of Amos Gilbert."

Gilbert stomped the gas pedal. Tires squealed, leaving a trail of black smoke. Professor Sparrow watched the truck fly down Rabbit Road. A smile unfurled the wrinkled face. "Mr. Amos Gilbert, as the Nobel-Prize-winning author, John Ernst Steinbeck, once said, *'Man is the only kind of varmint who sets his own trap, baits it, then steps in it.'* And you, my friend, have not seen the last of Benjamin Sparrow."

Morton greeted him at the kitchen door.

Meow.

The professor scratched his back. "Step one accomplished, ol' boy. Alice will come get you when I . . . vanish."

Meow.

"No complaining. If all goes as planned, we'll both be back home by Thanksgiving."

REFLECTIONS

POINT TO PONDER

Professor Sparrow _____ his own disappearance.
Have you ever made plans that didn't go as planned? What
were your plans? What happened?

PEARL FROM GOD

*"We can make our plans, but the LORD determines our
steps." (Proverbs 16:9)*

PRINCIPLE TO LIVE BY

Beloved, instead of taking your plans to God and asking
Him to bless them, go to God first and ask for His plans.
*"For I know the plans I have for you," says the LORD. "They
are plans for good and not for disaster, to give you a future
and a hope." (Jeremiah 29:11)*

Chapter 25:
As Planned

As Robert Burns penned in "To a Mouse," Professor Sparrow's *"best laid schemes"* did not go precisely as planned.

The professor disappeared — as planned.

Isaac asked Mrs. Alice for help — as planned.

Mrs. Alice delivered the first note — as planned.

The professor's disappearance made Amos Gilbert believe the old man had run off with the Confederate gold — as planned, which smoked the crooked rat out of his hiding hole — as planned.

Mrs. Alice planted the broken blue bottle pieces and two more messages — as planned.

The children put the puzzle pieces together — as planned.

HOWEVER . . .

The FBI coming on scene — not as planned.

Amos Gilbert shooting at the boys — most definitely not as planned.

The rat detaining and threatening the Fickles — categorically and unquestionably not as planned.

NONETHELESS . . .

Amos Gilbert's arrest and confession to first degree theft, unlawful use of a firearm, and harassment was plan accomplished. The rat got caught in his own trap — as planned.

And, finally, Isaac "Fish Fry" Fickle lost fear and found courage — as *God* planned.

7:27 P.M.

Moon shadows webbed Fairfax Road. Overhead, stars sparkled in the night sky like rhinestones on black velvet. Isaac pointed ahead. "Turn left up there, Dad."

Mr. Fickle hit the blinker. "Where are we going, buddy?

"To find Professor Sparrow. Hurry!"

Jacob shoved his brother. "Just tell us, Fish Fry."

Isaac grinned. "You'll see."

7:36 P.M.

The minivan pulled through tall gates. Headlights lit the driveway. Isaac jumped out of the van, raced up the hill, and around the old house, his family right on his heels. Lifting the flowerpot, the boy took the key and unlocked the door. In Professor Sparrow's kitchen, someone had . . .

Washed the cups and saucers up,

And brushed the crumbs away.

Swept the floor and made a fire

On that October day.

And settin' in his rocker,

Grinnin' ear to ear,

Professor Sparrow spouted out,

"Bout time you guys got here."

THE END

AFTERWORD

Dear Fisher,

Here's your book, Fish Fry — an action-packed adventure peppered with history, make believe, poetry, and notable quotes. I hope you like it. I had the "mostest" fun.

Granddaddy and I pray daily for you, Easton, Anya, Colt, Liam, Eli, and Luke, asking Jesus to grow all you grandkids into courageous servants of God. May each of you learn to stand strong and brave in every circumstance, going where God tells you to go, doing what God tells you to do, and always remembering that God is with you.

I love you *so* much!

Memaw